The Royal Diaries

Elisabeth

The Princess Bride

BY BARRY DENENBERG

Scholastic Inc. New York

Possenhofen, Bavaria
1853

Tuesday, July 12, 1853

Everyone has been in an <u>absolute frenzy</u> since Mama received Aunt Sophie's letter inviting her and Néné to visit next month. (Néné is my older sister — her real name is Helene, as mine is Elisabeth, although everyone calls me Sisi for reasons unknown to me.)

Of course it's not merely a <u>visit</u>, it's more a <u>command performance</u> since Mama always does what her older sister, the Archduchess, says. Aunt Sophie does have, shall we say, a rather imposing personality. The two of them have been discussing Néné's suitability as a match for Aunt Sophie's son, the Emperor. Mama is always alert for opportunities that will enhance the family's fortune.

The Emperor isn't his official title; that goes something like this:

Franz Joseph I, by the grace of God, Emperor of Austria, King of Hungary and Bohemia, King of Lombardy and Venice, of Dalmatia, Croatia, Slavonia, etc.; Archduke of Austria; Grand Duke of Tuscany and Cracow; Duke of Lorraine, Salzburg, Transylvania, and there's more, only no one can remember all of it, not even Mama.

When Mama read Aunt Sophie's letter out loud at breakfast I could see that Poppy had absolutely no intention of attending. For one thing, Poppy loathes pomp, pageantry, and all things royal, especially when they involve the Archduchess, the most royal of our many royal relatives.

Mama didn't want Poppy to come anyway because there is every likelihood that he would say something to offend Aunt Sophie (the two of them are even more incompatible than oil and water) and therefore, ruin Néné's chances of becoming Empress (or, more to the heart of the matter, ruin <u>Mama's</u> chances of becoming mama of the Empress).

I was very happy for my older sister but was eagerly looking forward to remaining behind with Poppy here at Possi. Then Mama got that gleam in her eye — the one that says she is planning something. She had the most fantastic idea: I should go along with them because the Emperor's younger brother, Archduke Karl Ludwig, would be there. According to Mama he had been "enthralled" (her word) with me ever since we first met at Innsbruck five years ago.

Mama, of course, would simply become prostrate with joy were she able to marry off two daughters for the price of one visit. Néné is, after all, only the beginning — Mama has four other girls who have to be properly paired off with appropriate husbands.

I was devastated that I wasn't going to be staying behind with Poppy. However, one cannot be sure that Poppy would, in fact, be staying at home, anyway.

And besides, one look at Mama was enough to convince me that protests, should I be foolish enough to voice them, would fall upon deaf ears.

I was going and that was that.

Tuesday, July 19, 1853

Besides not being with Poppy, my other regret is leaving my home at Possi even for such an auspicious occasion as witnessing my sister's engagement to the Emperor of Austria (although I must confess that the thought of missing all my piano lessons was a most welcome attraction).

The castle at Possenhofen — our Possi — is simply paradise, even if parts of the floors are crumbling, the staircase sways ominously from time to time, and there are those dreadful bats in the attic.

I don't care; I love it just the way it is. I always feel so happy and carefree when I am here. It is my castle in the country — complete with high towers at every corner and a moat. And there's so much else: swimming, fishing, mountain climbing, and hunting with Poppy and my older brothers. Walking in the late-summer garden when the roses have dropped their petals, creating the softest of blankets beneath my feet. The birds singing in the trees when I wake. The dreamlike morning mist on the lake, crisp autumn air, and the moonlight shining through the trees.

And, I almost forgot, the riding. Riding at Possi is simply the <u>best</u>. I ride my sweet Punch through the wooded park and along the lake, feeling the wind rushing through my hair. Stopping along the way, eating the berries until my lips turn purple, gathering wildflowers and tying them to my pommel before riding off again.

All my best pets are here: my roe deer, my guinea pigs, my rabbits and hamsters. I just love shooing all the mooing cows out of the rose garden and making sure the ponies don't ruin the lawns. And my dogs, my big, wonderful dogs running everywhere, getting their muddy paws on every couch, chair, divan, and ottoman in sight so that it is simply not possible to sit down without getting spittle or mud on one's clothing. All of which is most annoying to Mama but sheer delight as far as I am concerned.

And since we began spending Christmas here, it has become dearer to me still. Even though I know Christmas is celebrated by everyone all over the world, I can't help but think of it as my own personal holiday since I was born on Christmas Eve — 10:43 PM to be precise. For me it will always be mine and mine alone.

I remember the first Christmas we spent at Possi. Previously, we celebrated Christmas at our castle in Munich. Winter in Munich and summer in Possenhofen. Fortunately, it is only eighteen miles between the two. I enjoyed going back and forth — Mama is right, I do get bored easily. However, I much prefer the country to town.

I was nine when we began spending the most glorious Christmases at Possi.

That first Christmas, we had a snowball fight and then took a sleigh ride through the snow-laden forest and around the frozen winter lake. What a delight when we returned home, chilled to the bone, faces flushed, our magical castle transformed by the light from hundreds of candles.

We sat around the fire as the charred pine logs glowed orange, whooshing, hissing, and rolling over on themselves causing sprays of sparks to ascend while the chestnuts roasted. <u>Everyone</u> laughed, and there was toast after toast, goblets filled to overflowing with punch and held high, the glasses glittering, reflecting the light from the Christmas tree in the hall.

Poppy played his zither while the peasants from the surrounding area joined us for a dance (or two!). We <u>all</u> danced that first Christmas, even our newest family member, baby Sophie, who was tossed from arm to arm.

Sunday, July 24, 1853

Mama keeps asking me if I remember how sweet Karl Ludwig was, or how much he admired the cage of canaries I brought with me, or how he followed me everywhere and afterward wrote beautiful letters and sent the most extraordinary gifts: a watch on a chain, a dried rose, exotically colored butterflies mounted on a board, and gummy licorice whips.

I do remember Mama making sure I thanked him properly for each gift and answered each letter on my rose-colored stationery. Mama says I wrote a particularly charming note accompanied by one of my red ink sketches of my two pet lambs who loved me so much they followed me everywhere.

I remember the canaries and the lambs quite well but Karl Ludwig not quite so well, which exasperates Mama endlessly but makes perfect sense to me because I much prefer the company of animals to people.

The only thing I remember about Franz Joseph, who was not quite Emperor at the time, was that he pretty much ignored me the whole visit.

I do not even remember what he looked like. Mama says he is terribly attractive with blond hair, fine features, a slim figure, and impeccable military bearing. Mama says he is Europe's most eligible bachelor, although, she adds, not for long.

Tuesday, July 26, 1853

The house is filled with dressmakers, hatmakers, and shoemakers insisting on fittings and fluttering about like so many crazed moths to one overburdened flame — my poor sister. Mama wants to be sure that Néné has a sufficient number of satin gowns, velvet boots, and flower-trimmed bonnets.

Néné herself is more concerned with learning all the things that Aunt Sophie has informed Mama are <u>absolutely essential</u> if she wishes to make a good impression on the Emperor (which she does).

There are French lessons and dance lessons, including learning the polka and the mazurka since the Emperor is reportedly an excellent practitioner of both. Mama spends the whole day lecturing Néné about the sacrifices she will have to make, the responsibilities she will have to assume, and the obligations of a future Empress, which includes, it seems, learning to smile and chatter amiably even though one has nothing at all to say.

Néné is a serious and sensible young lady and is working hard to improve herself. Unfortunately, the one thing she will <u>never ever</u> be able to do is ride properly. (Unlike Poppy and I, Néné hates riding.) But she <u>has</u> to learn because Aunt Sophie has quite pointedly stated that "there is nothing the Emperor admires more in a woman than an elegant seat on a horse."

All anyone does lately is pay attention to Néné, which is quite all right with me. That way I am left to come and go as I please, daydreaming the day away.

Wednesday, July 27, 1853

Mama is angry that I was, once again, late for our compulsory 8:00 AM breakfast. I was helping Poppy with his oars — he was off fishing at dawn. Of course Néné was, as always, right on time. Néné is <u>very</u> punctual, like Mama. I'm more like Poppy: artistic, impulsive, gay, and poetic.

Poppy has his own pet name, Phantasius. Even when Poppy is merely talking about common, ordinary things, such as his desire that I try to improve my carriage, he says it poetically: "Sisi, you must learn to move like an angel with wings on your feet."

I write down all the poetic things Poppy says in my little velvet book, which I keep locked in a case at the bottom of my wardrobe. Besides this diary, it is my most precious possession.

Poppy is not only a talented poet but an accomplished playwright. His literary dining-club has grown to fourteen members (there are writers, musicians, and others of the like), and his circle grows wider with each passing year.

Poppy says that if we weren't princely born we could have been a riding act in the circus together, which would have pleased me greatly. Poppy even went so far as to build a circus behind our castle in Munich!

Once Poppy and I dressed up as strolling players and performed at a country wedding. Poppy sang and played and I danced, pigtails flying. When we were done, the applauding guests were so appreciative that they tossed copper coins, which I caught and gathered in my peasant's apron.

Unlike Mama and Néné, Poppy and I enjoy spending time with the coachmen, stable boys, foresters, and wood-cutters: the common people.

Poppy says when I was born I already had one tooth coming through just like Napolean, which, along with the fact that I am a Sunday's child, is a lucky omen.

> Monday's child is fair of face,
> Tuesday's child is full of grace,
> Wednesday's child is full of woe,
> Thursday's child has far to go,
> Friday's child is loving and giving,
> Saturday's child works hard for a living,
> But the child born on the sabbath day
> Is bonny and blythe, good and gay.

Bonny means beautiful.

I surprised Poppy with a poem of my own:

> I am Sunday's child, a child of the sun;
> Her golden rays she wove into my throne;
> With her glow she wove my crown;
> It is in her light that I live.

Friday, July 29, 1853

Néné is so angry with me that she has enlisted Mama's help. Mama's sense of humor — never one of her strong points (unlike Poppy) — has suffered lately due to the increasingly intensified preparations for the much-anticipated journey. With each passing day Mama is, I am afraid, losing all sense of proportion and balance. That is the only explanation I can offer in defense of her otherwise inexplicable decision to side with my sister.

Mama said I must immediately cease referring to Néné as the "Empress Helene" (that's her real name, Helene.) We almost all have other names besides the ones we were given upon birth. Four-year-old Max Emmanuel is "Mapperl" for reasons no one is sure of; Karl Theodor, two years younger than I, is "Gackel" because when he was little he cackled like a barnyard animal; Marie (twelve), Sophie (six), and my oldest brother, Ludwig, are just Marie, Sophie, and Ludwig, but ten-year-old Mathilde is "Spatz" because she's as gentle as a sparrow, or at least that's how the story goes. (Of course there's me, Sisi, and no one knows where that came from.)

Mama says "Her Serene and Most Royal Highness" is also quite unacceptable.

I don't see why Mama is so upset. After all, my sister _is_ going to become the Empress of Austria, which is as good as becoming "Empress of the Whole Entire World."

And she is most deserving of the honor. For one thing, she is my favorite of all my seven brothers and sisters. For another, she is quite attractive: tall, slender, and sharp featured. But her beauty is not only skin deep.

She is well educated, calm, poised, socially adept (unlike someone I know), a delightful companion, and a convivial conversationalist who can talk about whatever is called for by the occasion.

Tuesday, August 2, 1853

Mama is in a good frame of mind today because she received a rather lengthy letter from Aunt Sophie assuring her that Néné will make an absolutely wonderful Empress.

Wednesday, August 3, 1853

I do wish Poppy were coming with us. I miss him so when we are separated.

When we are apart I always carry around the same picture of him in my head. It is when he has his dreamy, faraway look. I like to look that way, too, so I practice in front of my mirror every day. It's quite unnerving, however, because every time I try to see if I am looking dreamy and faraway like Poppy, I find myself simply staring back at my own pupils.

Yesterday morning I laid down on the floor of Poppy's library and looked up at all the books he has. Poppy says he has 27,000 books but I simply do not believe him — he tends to exaggerate — so I have begun to count them. So far I've counted 187.

I keep wanting to ask him if he has read them all, but every time I think of it he's not here and, when he is, I have so many more important things to talk to him about that I just never remember to ask.

I was startled when he silently slipped into the library, but relieved to hear how proud he was when one of the peasants told him how I had jumped Punch over the high wall in the meadow, which no one has even <u>attempted</u> before or since. Or how I was thrown during one of my lessons and insisted on immediately remounting. He said I am one of the best students in our riding school.

Of course I never tell him that a great deal of that uncanny ability is due to the carrots and sugar I always carry in my pocket. The horses appreciate that I check on them every morning to make sure they are well-fed, properly groomed, rested, and above all, happy. After I am satisfied that is the case, I provide each one of them with a bit of sugar and carrot and a loving pat, pat, pat on the nose.

The house is always so melancholy when Poppy is away. This morning I thought I heard him whistling one of the latest music hall tunes (he knows them all), but although I ran up and down and this way and that trying to discover the source, he was nowhere to be found.

Néné said it must have been the wind, and, alas, I think she was right.

Of course it might have been him because one never knows when he might unexpectedly return from one of his expeditions or in whose company. When he returned from Asia Minor he had a raucous band following in his wake, and when he came back from Cairo — looking tanned and even handsomer than when he left — he brought home four little Negro boys that he had purchased in a slave market for us to play with, which caused quite a stir.

Frankly, I think Poppy likes to surround himself in a veil of mystery.

Mama blames his lack of discipline for my restlessness. I heard them arguing about it in the library. (The argument was about when my governess, Baroness Wulfen, tied me to a chair and told Mama it was because I didn't sit still for one single, solitary moment all day long. That just wasn't true. I sat perfectly still the whole time, sketching the lake and the snowcapped mountain peaks. I am perfectly capable of sitting still if I like what I am doing. If I don't, I can't, and I defy anyone to explain to me what precisely is wrong with that.)

After that, Poppy interrupted my lessons so he could teach me to ride bareback like the gypsy children. Mama said Poppy's "artistic nonsense" was the cause of my "whims." According to Mama I spend more time in my own imagination than with my feet planted firmly on the ground, where they belong. Even if that's true — which

I'm not sure it is — I think Mama has never considered that perhaps life in my imagination is more interesting than life with both feet firmly planted on the ground.

When Mama is not scolding me for being nervous and easily distracted, she tells me I brood too much, which means I don't tell her, on a moment-by-moment basis, every thought — no matter how fleeting or trivial or private — that floats through my mind.

I wish Mama would not complain so much about Poppy. I would rather not take sides but Mama does seem overly sensitive, although she is right about Poppy being a flirt.

However she has only herself to blame because she has forgiven Poppy's eccentricities and transgressions time and time again. His insistence on spending noontime with his "other children" (that is to say, children who are not Mama's) is troubling and she most certainly has a right to be chagrined.

But I don't see that as a reason to allow the entire structure of the family to deteriorate to the point where they don't speak to each other even when passing in the halls.

Or worse, allowing what happened this winter: When we were home in Munich, Mama got so angry that we had to move to a separate part of the palace just so she did not have to see Poppy!

Saturday, August 6, 1853

I don't have nearly as much to pack as my sister and Mama. Everything fits quite nicely into my small canvas satchel.

Mama has always made packing a more arduous and odious task than necessary and this time is no exception.

First, she has to compile a list of everything she's taking: frocks, bonnets, petticoats, camisoles, kerchiefs, lap robes, hosiery, fans (her everyday parchment one and the lace one for balls), smelling salts and headache powders (possibly the most important items), patent leather boots, and her prayer book.

She insists on packing everything herself and then calling poor Gustav, the valet, when the wicker portmanteau is stuffed to overflowing.

Tuesday, August 9, 1853

Néné and I had a long, sister-to-sister talk about her momentous, upcoming meeting. We leave in only two days!

Néné seems quite composed, at least for all outward appearances; however, if you know her as well as I do you can see that she is, in fact, quite agitated and apprehensive.

I am glad she chose to unburden herself to me. She went on for quite a while. She said that if she has to jam one more historical fact, guideline of appropriate behavior, description of proper procedures, or rule concerning what to talk about and what not to, she believes her head will surely burst at the seams (although I am not sure if a head actually has seams).

Ever since we received Aunt Sophie's invitation to the royal family's summer residence this is all poor Néné has thought about. She is terrified that if she says or does the wrong thing it will all come to naught.

I assured her she would do fine, which I truly believe, and urged her not to be so concerned with what everyone thinks, which is difficult for her because that's just the way she is.

She laughed, which I thought was a very good sign, and said that was easy for me to say because I don't care what other people think, and although that was not entirely accurate, I understood her sentiment.

She said she wished she could be honest like me and be more at ease telling people how she feels. She also said she wished she had my natural beauty and easy charm, which is simply ridiculous because Néné is justly considered the beauty of the family, and, as far as charm is concerned, I don't really think I have any — all of which I said to her.

She put her arm around me and said that I no longer looked like her shy, little baby sister but more like a radiant young lady.

She pointed out how the shape of my face was changing in the most flattering way (I hadn't really noticed) and how my hair had turned from golden-blond to the most attractive shade of auburn, and commented favorably about how long it has gotten. (When undone, it now reaches all the way to the back of my knees! The only problem is that it takes hours each day just to fix it properly. Despite that, I know that I will never, ever cut my hair, which is my finest feature.)

If only my teeth weren't so appalling. I was so embarrassed last night when Mama, who utterly lacks discretion sometimes, mentioned their dreadful condition at dinner. (I had to stop myself from blurting out that it was not I who was going to be presented to the Emperor for his approval.)

I decided right then and there not to smile or laugh when I am around anyone during the <u>entire</u> visit. This morning I began teaching myself to talk without parting my lips, which is most difficult and can only be done if I whisper.

And I have also made a solemn promise to myself that I will watch every morsel of food that goes into my mouth. I will not eat too much and grow fat as a tub right before everyone's astonished eyes.

Wednesday, August 10, 1853

I know Mama is worried that she will never find me a proper husband, even though she admits it's a little too early to panic. According to Mama, who is invariably right about these things, eighteen, which just happens to be

Néné's age, is the <u>perfect</u> age to marry. Somehow when Mama talks about the perfect age to marry I picture a ripe fruit being passed over, and I worry that, like an overripe fruit, I will languish, alone, forgotten, and misshapen. Mama keeps telling me I am too young but she appeared quite dismayed when things did not work out with her plans for me this past spring.

Néné says I shouldn't give any of this a moment's thought. She is certain I will find someone as she has, although we both laughed when I said, "Not an Emperor." Néné believes I will find someone very, very soon. She says she can feel it in her heart.

Of course the conversation revealed more about what my sister wasn't saying than what she was. She wasn't saying anything about what happened with Count Richard S—— (even now — even in my own private diary — I don't dare write his full name).

To this day, I don't know how anyone found out that I had his portrait or that I spent countless hours hiding behind that hedge hoping to catch a glimpse of him.

I was questioned like a common criminal, although I revealed nothing, and never will.

Then suddenly, he was gone! Vanished. Banished. Off somewhere, they said, although they never said where or why and for how long. "Unsuitable," Mama muttered, and Poppy said nothing.

As if that weren't enough to endure, he returned just as suddenly as when he left and then became gravely ill and died!

There was absolutely no one to talk to. Only writing my poems and riding my ponies provided any solace for my broken heart. Only they aided me in my desperate attempt to extinguish the inferno of my blazing anguish.

I spent countless hours locked in my room at my writing table, weeping and composing my secret poems:

> Once more the die has fallen
> and Richard is no more

When I am deeply disturbed and that feeling of helplessness and hopelessness overwhelms me, nothing calms my fears more soothingly than composing a poem.

Somehow — and it is truly a mystery to me — transporting my melancholy thoughts from inside me to the paper before me magically lessens my heavy burden. Miraculously, once I have taken pen in hand, the burden is no longer mine alone. And the poem so often expresses thoughts and feelings that I didn't even realize I possessed.

I hope someday to be a poet, like Poppy. It is from him that I have my poetic nature.

When I was so weary and overwrought I could write no more, I rode. The faster I rode, the further behind my troubles appeared until, finally, I galloped hard enough and far enough that they diminished to the point of tolerability.

Mama is hoping — I know just how she thinks — that this trip will help me forget the Count. But I will never forget. Never.

Monday, August 15, 1853
Bad Ischl, Austria

Although I adore traveling, I cannot say our journey has been a pleasant one.

Néné sat so rigidly in the carriage during the first part of the trip that I had to look to see if she was blinking, fearing that she had simply frozen into an upright position.

I tried my best to be cheerful and distract her, but she and Mama contributed so little to the conversation that I asked them if they wished me to cease my endless prattle so everyone could ride enveloped in their own private silence, which appeared is what they desired.

Mama didn't respond, already in the throes of a migraine, but Néné begged me to go on, assuring me that my stories were quite delightful and entertaining and were indeed the only thing helping keep her mind off her infinite concerns.

Mama criticized me for one thing or another for most of the trip. When she wasn't correcting my behavior, she was giving me one of her angry glances, although sometimes it's hard to tell if it's me or the migraine that's bothering her.

She lectured me about being more aware of my exalted position in life and reminded me that I was born a girl and not a boy and that I should start behaving in a ladylike fashion.

She was upset that I was entirely too familiar with Nandl. (It annoys Mama that I, like Poppy, would stoop to converse with a common person like the carriage attendant. She would be even more annoyed if she knew how much more interesting and informative I find them than the numerous royals we so often have as guests.)

She wanted me to call him by his proper name, Herr Ferdinand, and stop poking him in the ribs.

She was also upset that I fell into the horse-drinking trough when we stopped at an inn to rest our weary bones and our even more weary horses. It wasn't all my fault, however. Partly the horses were to blame. They were exceedingly thirsty and were neighing, snorting, and tossing their heads to show their impatience, and as I was leading one of them to the trough, I slipped and fell head over heels back into the dangerously low trough. I didn't fall in all the way, but enough to wet my dress. It was really quite funny, although Mama failed to see any humor in it at all, which she made quite clear.

Nandl — I mean, Herr Ferdinand — helped me wipe most of the horse spittle off my dress but there was little we could do about the mud on my boots. Mama threatened to send me back home by the noon post, but instead made me sit on the top of the cart with Fräulein Rödi, which she thought would be punishment enough.

Frankly, that was fine with me because Fräulein Rödi was entirely better company than either Mama or my sister.

Somehow we managed to become separated from our baggage coach (with all of our dresses) and our ladies-in-waiting. Due to the tardiness of our arrival and the vexing problem of the missing coach, we will be unable to change clothes so we all must meet the Emperor wearing the mourning dresses we traveled in. (We are mourning the passing of our aunt — not, of course, Aunt Sophie, who is very much alive and very much annoyed by the lateness of our arrival.)

One can only hope the Emperor likes black.

Mama's dreadful state was not improved by the fact that Aunt Sophie did not come to greet us at the hotel herself but sent instead one of her ladies-in-waiting, although she was kind enough to reserve the proper rooms for us.

Néné grew paler by the minute. She was understandably glum because she was going to have to meet her prospective husband wearing her now quite dusty black dress and feels that she doesn't look good in black. (Rightly so, I have to admit, as Néné's complexion is generally sallow.)

Thankfully, my hair looks good. One of Aunt Sophie's

maids fixed it quite nicely in two, simple, long braids with a large comb holding them away from my face.

We're off to meet the Emperor.

Tuesday, August 16, 1853

Although I am still thoroughly fatigued from the trying journey, I am even more exhausted after being buffeted about by the endless whirlwind of events that are swirling around me.

I have to steel myself to remain awake long enough to record at least the bare bones of what has transpired thus far.

Frankly, I don't know what to make of it all or if, in fact, I am making something of nothing. Usually I can talk to Néné when things are this confusing, but that is simply out of the question here.

So much has happened in such an abbreviated amount of time — can it be that I have only been here a matter of hours and not days or weeks? It is utterly impossible to catch one's breath long enough to light on a single, solitary moment.

In just one day I have <u>met</u> more people than I have <u>seen</u> in my entire fifteen years of living and breathing on this earth. Nearly all of them are complete and total strangers whose names I forget just as soon as I hear them.

It is most distressing and periodically I want to run away and hide.

I must confess that meeting the Emperor was quite stimulating. I was anticipating it with fear and trembling, but he received us in his mother's drawing room at their lovely villa and was most charming. I was quite relieved that he remembered me (at least he said he did), and I was even more relieved that he appeared pleased to see me.

We spoke only briefly and I confess to being the tiniest bit disappointed that he talked to me like I was a little girl, although I suppose to someone as old as he is — he will be twenty-three in just two days — I must seem terribly young.

Frankly, and most confidentially, I had the distinct impression that he was being quite playful, even teasing me. Of course I could be mistaken about this latter observation.

He appeared to have recovered most miraculously from the anarchist's dagger attack last year. Poppy says that if the Emperor hadn't turned his neck at just the right moment (what Poppy refers to as "in the neck of time") the knife would have pierced him mortally rather than being deflected by the gold embroidery of his military jacket collar.

Despite his gaily decorated uniform, his military posture, and spurs that jangled when he walked, he did not seem nearly as austere and forbidding as I thought he would be. And he was surprisingly and infinitely more handsome than I had remembered, although my memories are quite vague since I was only ten years old when I first met him.

Mama, whose migraine was diminished, chatted merrily with her sisters, Aunt Sophie and Queen Elise of Prussia, which, I must say, was something of a relief from the unbearable tension. The atmosphere was so stiff and so formal and everyone was pretending so hard to talk about everything and anything under the sun other than the real reason we were gathered there.

And no one, of course, was more painfully aware of this than my dear, sweet sister who looked positively stricken. Her lips were pressed together so tightly it looked like she was being tortured rather than being introduced to her future husband.

She looked so ill at ease, so out of place: like someone who had accidentally made a wrong turn and entered the wrong room and was wondering who all these people were and where were the people <u>she</u> knew and was supposed to be with.

She was still upset that our dresses had not arrived with us so she could change into something more colorful, gay, and flattering. Néné does look so lovely in the right things.

I spoke to dear, sweet Karl Ludwig. He's eighteen already! He was quite overjoyed to see me, which made me feel more comfortable.

He is not nearly as shy as he was the last time we met, which I was bold enough to mention to him. He returned the compliment and said that I, too, had changed and quite for the better. I could see that he meant it most truly.

He seemed content to remain in my company, telling me the wittiest jokes and whispering incidentals in my ear. He has saved all of my letters. He was constantly offering me cakes and ices that I declined just as rapidly and repeatedly as they were offered to me.

While I was talking to Karl Ludwig I couldn't help but steal a glance from time to time at his older brother. Much to my bewilderment, each time I did this the Emperor appeared to be doing the <u>exact same thing</u>.

He was staring at me in the most intense manner, as if there were something quite important and urgent that he had forgotten to tell me when we talked so briefly earlier, but because of the milling crowd, each and every person vying for his and only his attention, he could not fathom how he was going to be able to approach me in order to broach this most pressing matter.

This went on for some time and I must admit it made me feel embarrassed. I could sense the blood pulsing through my veins, coursing up my neck, and enveloping my face like tendrils wrapping themselves around a tree that was too weak to resist and too rooted to the ground to move out of harm's way.

I discreetly tried shaking my head and blinking my eyes to see if that would help the mirage before my eyes disappear or wake me from the vexing but most curiously pleasant dream I was having. But it was clearly no dream because when I stopped shaking and blinking, there, just as before, were his eyes on mine.

I tried paying closer attention to what Karl Ludwig was saying in hopes that the next time I looked at the Emperor he would be deeply engrossed in some kind of incredibly important conversation involving matters of state, but each time I did that I found his eyes still on mine, save only that he had moved to another position in the room.

I thought I was being rather clever and circumspect about all of this but I don't think I was quite as clever nor quite as circumspect as I thought because Karl Ludwig appeared to be growing quite distressed and, unless I am mistaken, jealous (although he said nothing).

I fear that tomorrow will be just as unnerving and chaotic as today.

Wednesday, August 17, 1853

Rather than think the world was spinning around a little too fast yesterday, I should have been content to count my blessings for yesterday's torrid pace has been increased tenfold!

The afternoon was, thankfully, most uneventful. The

Emperor spent the day with his mother, although he did cancel his plans to go hunting, which, speculation has it, was a most unusual occurrence (and deemed to be full of meaning).

Mama, due to the regrettable return of her migraine, was unable to attend dinner but allowed me to stay up. I was so excited I could hardly eat, which was just as well because I could feel my waist expanding as a result merely of <u>watching</u> everyone else gobble down their food.

As indicated by my place card, I sat next to the Prince of Hesse. Noting my still-full plate, the Prince inquired if I were fasting for some reason. This was the most humorous sentence he uttered all evening, remaining throughout blissfully unaware of how boring he was.

Sitting next to him was so unrelentingly uninteresting that I began to search around for more compelling places to place my attention and finally settled on my sister and her soon-to-be intended.

They were sitting quite far away — Néné in the place of honor between the Emperor and his father. Most distressingly, they appeared to be saying little to each other, lapsing mostly into what appeared to be embarrassingly long silences.

Even more distressing was the fact, which I couldn't help but notice, that the Emperor continued to look at me much as he had earlier, despite the immediate presence of my sister.

I wish he had been a little less bold but he is, after all, the Emperor and, I imagine, can stare at anyone he wants. I wondered if anyone else at the table was taking note of this most disturbing development but was afraid to look.

It took forever to dress for the ball, which, at the Emperor's insistence, I was now required to attend. Néné wore her white silk gown with a garland of ivy wrapped around her brow. I wore my peach voile and had my hair done with a diamond arrow pinned within my curls, a perfect final touch.

There were hundreds of guests already assembled by the time we arrived and all of them were looking at me. Of course they had probably been looking at me all day and all during dinner but now they were being so bold about it I couldn't help but notice. It was as if they couldn't take their eyes off of me, fearing that if they did, no matter how briefly, they might miss some momentous event.

Everyone was chattering away about how disappointing it was that, due to the cold and the rain, we would be unable to dance out on the lawn and how that has caused the most overcrowded situation in the villa.

As if I weren't nervous enough, the Emperor indicated that he wished me to come sit beside him, which of course I did.

Then Major Baron something-or-other, the Emperor's aide-de-camp, crossed the floor, approached, bowed, and asked me to dance a polka, which I think he was put up to by Aunt Sophie so the Emperor could see if I knew how to dance properly.

I must admit that I felt lighter on my feet than I thought I would, due, in large part, to the Baron's expert leadership.

The Emperor — just as I suspected — watched closely as if judging my ability in this category as he had already in the others.

I told the Major Baron that I didn't know if I would be able to get through the cotillion without the assistance of my dancing instructor who, alas, was unable to accompany us on the journey.

Sensing my apprehension he assured me, in a soothing tone of voice, that he was certain everything would turn out fine in the end. I could not be sure if he was commenting on the ball or had in mind some other, perhaps larger and more vexing, problem. And how could he be so certain everything would turn out fine in the end? Did he know something I did not? Did everyone?

He complimented me on the musical nature of my dancing and my ability to keep time, although I think he was mostly trying to be kind.

When the dance ended, on my way to the punch bowl, I overheard him whisper to a compatriot, "I suspect I have been dancing with the future Empress." I know that made me blush enormously although, regrettably, there was no mirror close at hand. It was the first time such an overwhelming and inconceivable idea had entered my head.

After my dance with the Baron, the Emperor barely left my side for the rest of the evening. Then my worst fear materialized! It was nearly midnight when the Emperor asked me to dance. I was pleased beyond description that I did not fall down and embarrass myself in front of him and this most distinguished audience.

I could feel his arms around my waist, gentle but self-assured, as he waltzed me around the room. All I could think was that these were the arms of the Emperor of Austria! I closed my eyes briefly, hoping that would allow me to maintain my composure. When I opened them I realized we were the only ones dancing. Everyone else was standing and watching us.

When the dance ended, the Emperor presented me with a bouquet of flowers, which I thought was a lovely gesture.

Mama has since explained to me that it means he has chosen me to be his wife!

Thursday, August 18, 1853

It is best, I think, to begin at the beginning and proceed ever so slowly in order to be certain not to leave anything out. Then, at the end, when I'm done writing it all down, I can read it back to myself to see if what I think has happened has actually happened.

In the morning it rained so hard it was simply impossible to go out so I slept late, which was most beneficial. I was exceedingly tired from staying up so late last night recording everything in my diary, and, even after I finally laid my head on the pillow, I had a restless night's sleep.

Most of what follows I learned from a source whose

identity I am unable to reveal even in the privacy of my own diary. I am thoroughly convinced of the impeccable reputation of that unnamed person and the unimpeachable nature of the information provided.

The source reported that the Emperor was unable to sleep, so anxious was he to speak to his mother concerning a matter of the utmost personal importance. The Emperor was so impatient that he could only bring himself with the greatest of efforts to wait for her to wake. When Aunt Sophie did wake she was, it turns out, suffering from a debilitating migraine. (Migraines seem to run in Mama's family.) Her migraine notwithstanding, she suffered to receive her son, who was beaming with happiness and nearly bursting with anticipation.

He explained to his mother that it was I he found most attractive!

He then went on at some length: I had a magnificent crown of hair (my hair has looked particularly good these past two days); I was refreshing, exuberant, and youthful. He saw the sweetest look in my light brown eyes and my lips were as soft and as inviting as ripe strawberries! I was like a rosebud that opened under the rays of the morning sun!

Those were his <u>exact words</u>.

Aunt Sophie could plainly see that her son was smitten. She herself was quite stunned by the effusive nature of his pronouncements, seeing as he had not been, heretofore, of such a poetic bent.

She paused, considering carefully how to respond to this unprecedented (but not completely unexpected, given what had transpired over the past forty-eight hours) outpouring.

She reminded her son that <u>Helene</u> and not I was to be his intended and that I couldn't possibly be considered a suitable match because I was still a mere child.

She cautioned him to consider carefully. There was no hurry to decide. He needn't act rashly. "Make haste slowly," she said.

Aunt Sophie went on in this vein at some length, urging him to reexamine Helene perhaps more closely. She pointed out how sensitive, charming, attractive, and poised Helene was, emphasizing the last characteristic as one essential for anyone hoping to become Empress of Austria (and implying that I had none of these characteristics).

He was not, she reminded him, an ordinary man. He was the Emperor and his duty and responsibilities were to God.

The Emperor remained unbowed and unrepentant.

Respectfully, but steadfastly, he explained that although he could see that Helene had many, many virtues, including all of those mentioned, she was a little too grave for his taste.

Frankly, I was at this point so taken aback by this quite unexpected recounting that I made my source repeat it for me more slowly and assure me that she wasn't suffering from some strange malady that might cause her to be in a state of confusion, a state that perhaps included imagined conversations.

She understandably took exception to this but swore an oath that every word she spoke was the Lord's truth.

Having put my doubts to rest I urged her to continue.

The Emperor wanted Aunt Sophie to speak to Mama, requesting my hand in marriage!

I was not, he emphasized, to be coerced in any way and it was to be conveyed to me that he was most acutely aware that, due to his position, sharing his life would put great responsibilities on me, and if I were unwilling to accept those responsibilities he would truly understand.

This was, of course, most kind and considerate of the Emperor. He is such a dear, sweet man. I only wish he were not the Emperor — then I wouldn't be nearly as apprehensive as I am. It is the Emperor I fear marrying, not Franz Joseph.

Although I was nearly overcome with happiness, I was at the same time plagued by the odious question of what on earth I was going to say to my sister. I was nearly paralyzed with fear by the prospect of speaking to her about this most perverse distortion of our plans.

This is the very first time <u>anything</u> has come between us. I cherish our relationship so. Néné is the only one I can <u>always, always</u> count on.

I know full well what Néné will do. She will do what she always does when she is agitated: She will speak volumes about everything under the sun, pretending with fervor and conviction that nothing in the world is the matter.

I tremble at the thought of facing her.

But I had no time for this or any other feelings. The

day was unfolding at its own pace — as if with a will of its own. I was forced onto center stage, compelled to play the starring role in a play I had not read, until I discovered wherein resided my destiny.

The Emperor requested that I assume the place of honor next to him. Néné sat at the far end of the table, where I had sat just hours earlier. This placement was fortunate because we could avoid speaking to or even looking at each other at so public an occasion.

There were numerous toasts to the Emperor's health and in recognition of his birthday. He was most talkative and gay throughout the meal. I ate with a healthy appetite because I thought that would please him (it did), and he appeared proud to have me by his side. Strangely, I did not feel intimidated or uncomfortable with him — only with all the people who constantly surround him like satellite planets around a sun.

The weather improved somewhat after lunch so we went for a brief excursion in a closed barouche through the forest to Wolfgang. As I predicted, Néné talked the whole way in a most animated and artificial manner.

The Emperor looked exceptionally handsome to me at

that moment. His blue eyes, attractive blond hair, well-shaped eyebrows, sensitive lips, and infectious laugh, all absolutely essential characteristics, were most appealing.

I am afraid we acted in a most insensitive manner, gazing the whole time into each other's eyes, oblivious of Aunt Sophie and Néné and making no attempt to hide our mutual feelings.

After the drive we had tea and then, in the early evening, Mama came to me, looking quite apprehensive. I had, of course, by then spoken with my source and knowing what Mama needed to say, I decided to relieve her of her burden. I told her I already knew what she had come to speak to me about.

Mama was so relieved she might have fallen on the floor had she not been so eager to hear my reaction.

I told her I was quite fond of the Emperor. She asked me if I could love him, and I asked, "How could anyone not love that man?" surprising myself by the depths of my feelings at this very emotional moment.

Overwhelmed, I burst into tears and vowed I would do everything in my power to make the Emperor happy and be a loving child to dear Aunt Sophie.

When I told Mama I was deeply concerned about

Néné, she insisted we had no time for that. "One does not send the Emperor of Austria packing" was how Mama so delicately put it. Mama was clearly overjoyed that the trip had not been a waste and had, due to the most unexpected of twists, turned out to be a success. She had, after all, accomplished her mission, which was to marry one of her daughters to the Emperor of Austria. If the particular daughter she had in mind didn't work out but another one did, it was of little consequence to her.

Without another word about my sister, Mama sat down to write a note accepting the Emperor's proposal.

Sunday, August 21, 1853

The Emperor appeared at our hotel early this morning and waited outside our room until he could see me. Aunt Sophie had already received Mama's note and shown it to him. It was the first time we were completely alone. (He is always surrounded by people, and I wonder if he ever spends even one minute in solitude.) Sadly, the time was all too brief, although I was pleased to notice that I did not feel nearly as afraid as I thought I would.

The Emperor most graciously offered me his arm and escorted me to breakfast where we were joined by his family — Karl Ludwig looked near tears — and the imperial entourage, all of whom kept stealing glances at me.

Mama had already sent a telegram to Poppy, which read: "The Emperor has asked for Sisi's hand in marriage and awaits your consent. He is staying in Ischl until the end of August. We are all blissfully happy."

Of course we were not <u>all</u> blissfully happy, but Mama made no mention of that either in the telegram or during our daily discourse, which was just as well.

The weather was glorious and at eleven we proceeded to church to attend Mass. I wore my simple, sprigged muslin dress and a charming, wide-brimmed leghorn straw hat.

Upon descending the carriage, the Emperor, who is always most attentive, once again offered me his arm. We entered the church, which was filled to overflowing with people. I was most startled by Aunt Sophie's insistence that I enter before her. At the time I did not fully understand the true meaning of this, but Mama later explained that it was Aunt Sophie's humble way of acknowledging my future role: As Empress I would be higher in rank than my aunt, the Archduchess.

The priest was moved to tears when the Emperor said, "Will Your Reverence please give us your blessing, for this is my future wife." Then the priest blessed us both.

When I turned to leave, out of the corner of my eye I caught my sister's face and could draw no conclusions about what she was thinking that moment from her visage, which appeared sad but guarded.

I hardly spoke a word at the banquet and official reception that followed. I met even more people there — courtiers and the ladies who attended to Aunt Sophie — all of whom insisted on kissing my hand. The Emperor's aide, Count Grunne, gave a speech in our honor.

When we exited, the crowds — all of them jostling for a better view — had spilled out of the church and into the surrounding streets. The shops had opened especially to celebrate this occasion and displayed the blue-and-white ribbons of Bavaria, which fluttered from the rooftops and windows along with the yellow-and-black banners of the Emperor's Imperial House of Habsburg.

Throughout the town, everyone was shouting my name

and appeared to be in a rapturous frenzy that was terrifying and exhilarating all at once. I was in tears nearly the whole time: tears of joy, tears of sadness, tears of apprehension.

Tuesday, August 30, 1853

Tomorrow we leave to return to Possi!

I have been grateful for all the activity that has distracted me these last few days: a shooting expedition in the mountains, picnics, an outdoor supper on the barge, and a fantastic fireworks display. (Poor, dear Aunt Sophie had to remain in her bedroom because the noise was making her too nervous.) They permitted me some respite from my myriad concerns: What will I say to Néné? What will it be like to be married? How will I ever learn to become an Empress? What will it be like to live in Vienna?

Only seeing how happy the Emperor is in my presence assures me that our course of action is the proper one. The only one. Each day he seemed more delighted with me than the one before, never tiring of my company. Even when I had to sit for hours and hours having my portrait done, the Emperor insisted on remaining by my side the entire time. (It was an endlessly tedious task — Mama says that patience is a virtue but frankly I don't see why.) I was not very good company I'm afraid, since I had to sit there and concentrate on not moving. The Emperor glowed like a candle when the artist said I had the loveliest face he had ever painted.

Each day the Emperor showered me with gifts, one lovelier than the next, my favorite being a tendril of diamonds and emeralds that can be braided into my hair.

At dinner, he taught me how to lift my glass by the stem rather than the part that holds the liquid so that my fingers don't muffle the sound of the clinking glasses during the toasts. The Emperor is so sweet and thoughtful that he even put up a swing in the garden just for me!

Poppy came just as soon as he received the telegram. He has been proud as a peacock ever since.

The only constant cloud on the horizon is Néné, who is an endless cause for concern. She keeps to herself, speaking to me as little as possible and never looking at me. Every time I approach her (after two attempts I ceased) she puts her fingers to her lips signaling that she would prefer my silence to my words of explanation, and so there it remains.

Mama says that Néné is convinced that the Emperor rejected her because she is eighteen and, therefore, too old to marry. Now she thinks it is too late for her to find anyone suitable.

Even Aunt Sophie's most generous gift, a cross of diamonds and turquoise, hasn't improved Néné's grim demeanor. I must admit she has been less grim these past two days but that is because she knows we are soon leaving. She has been longing to go home almost the whole time we have been here.

The Emperor is nearly as sad as I am about tomorrow. He is most distressed that he has to return to the pile of official state papers that surely await atop his work desk. He vows he will visit soon, which has made our impending separation tolerable, but only barely so.

Thursday, September 8, 1853
Possenhofen, Bavaria

Ever since I returned home I have tried to hold fast to the memory of those magical moments when I first met the Emperor. It is difficult, however, as each day they slip further and further from my grasp until by now, they have already begun to fade, disappearing slowly behind the fog of time.

Has all this really happened, I ask myself, or have I merely dreamed it?

Fortunately, almost every day a letter from the Emperor arrives confirming that I have not been dreaming. He writes the most considerate letters, telling me again and again how wondrous our meeting in Ischl was: Our "divine sojourn," he calls it.

He is right; it was truly divine.

Friday, September 9, 1853

At last Néné and I have spoken. As I anticipated, Néné regained her composure and began chatting amiably once we were home. Amiably with everyone but me, that is. I wanted so much to speak to her <u>truly</u> but couldn't allow myself, afraid she would, once again, reject my overtures.

Finally, she responded when I approached her about small matters. I used English, our secret language. No one else understands English so it has become our habit to speak it when we don't want anyone around to understand what we are talking about. It made me feel that we still had something special between us, as before, even if the subject was trivial.

I wanted to go a step further and broach the unspeakable subject that has so odiously come between us. However, I could see from the look in my sister's eyes that the time for that had not yet come.

Saturday, September 10, 1853

Every time I turn around there is another luxurious gift arriving from the Emperor's Habsburg relatives: furs, silks, jewelry. Today an exquisite ivory-bound prayer book arrived.

Wednesday, September 21, 1853

Another letter from the Emperor.

He cannot wait until he is free from his dreary official

duties and obligations so he can join me here at Possi. He has a portrait of me right by his writing table and shows it to everyone he sees.

I so look forward to his visit. When we are apart I worry about the wisdom of our plans.

Saturday, September 24, 1853

Finding myself the most important person in the whole household and the constant center of attention is most unnerving and disturbing. I wish it were not so, but there doesn't seem to be anything I can do to stop it.

I can't go out anywhere unless everyone knows where I am because there are so many great personages and foreign delegations arriving night and day to meet me. Although they mean well, their speeches are so long that the mere anticipation of one is enough to ruin my entire day.

Possi used to be so serene and calming. Now that I have so much to do, it is far from that. I hardly have any time to spend with my animals, walk in the woods, or even ride with Poppy.

I wish I could go back to the way things were, before

Ischl. (Except, of course, I would never give up meeting the Emperor!) Then no one cared where I was or when I was going to be back. And there were no foreign delegations coming to meet me.

Now I am hardly ever alone.

Monday, September 26, 1853

A courier came today with a miniature of the Emperor that was painted at Ischl and set in a diamond bracelet. It is simply lovely.

The Emperor said he will be here in mid-October. I have already begun counting the days.

Thursday, September 29, 1853

Aunt Sophie sent a sketch of the Emperor and me that was made when we were in Ischl. It was most thoughtful of her.

She has decided to buy the villa that they were renting in Ischl and make it a permanent summer imperial villa.

But that's not all: She is going to have a new wing built in the shape of an E for me, Elisabeth!

Friday, October 7, 1853

Fräulein Rödi said that we have to get a special dispensation from the Pope in order to be properly married. It sounded most ominous and foreboding but Fräulein Rödi says it is a mere formality and nothing to concern myself about. She said it is because the Emperor and I are cousins, but Mama and Poppy are cousins so it is perfectly all right.

Thursday, October 13, 1853

At last, the Emperor has come.

He said the trip was most arduous and took much longer than expected. He visited the King in Munich before arriving here yesterday. He was so happy to see me that I was blushing the whole day. He acted more like a boy than an Emperor, which was most refreshing to see. He played with Mapperl and Sophie and said it was good to forget his responsibilities, if even for a brief time. I told him I was glad that I could provide that respite for him.

I was relieved to see that Néné, too, was most delighted to see the Emperor and gave him a heartfelt welcome. In the evening, she danced with one of the Emperor's handsome aides.

Although we are not the way we once were, I do feel that we are both doing our best to mend the torn fabric of our sisterly relationship. It is a great gratification to me that we are once again talking like we did before and that Néné is showing signs of returning to her old self.

Friday, October 14, 1853

Although August in Ischl will always have a special place in my heart, I am enjoying our time together even more now. I feel more like myself.

The Emperor mentioned that he noticed the difference and he approves.

Monday, October 17, 1853

The Emperor admired my balance in the saddle and was surprised by how well I rode. I, for my part, was surprised to see that he is able to mount his horse almost as quickly as I am.

Riding alongside him is pure pleasure. Sometimes he speeds up and gallops ahead and then stops and waits for me. He so enjoys thinking he is the superior horseman that I let him go on thinking that. Then we slow the horses down to a walk so we can hold hands, just the two of us, all alone.

I was relieved that the Emperor did not mention Aunt Sophie's concern that my teeth were too yellow (she has told Mama that I ought to take better care of them) and that I ride too much — a concern that she did press upon Mama. Of course Mama knows that there is no such thing as riding too much and that nothing gives me as much pleasure.

The Emperor said my riding seems to be doing wonders for my constitution, which is quite true. I think he said that because I am not nearly as slender as I was when we met in August and he approves. I can see that he is pleased that my teeth are much whiter now thanks to the care I have been taking with them (although he was much too polite to say anything, of course).

He was also pleased that I have made such a good impression on everyone. According to him, my charms are being widely praised.

I would prefer he not mention things like that. I hate thinking about whether or not people approve of me — like I am an object to be considered for purchase and not flesh and blood like them.

Wednesday, October 19, 1853

We all went to Munich to celebrate Queen Marie's birthday, which was quite an opulent affair.

When we entered our box at the theater, everyone stood up at once and cheered in honor of our upcoming marriage. There was a performance of the *William Tell Overture* scheduled but the King ordered it withdrawn because he most strongly disapproved of the plot.

Thursday, October 20, 1853

Balls, balls, balls.

What did I do with all of my time before I had to attend all these balls? Mama says that attending balls and banquets and receiving diplomats and delegations (in the appropriate local costumes) is the order of the day in Vienna and I'd best get used to it. With each passing day, Mama adds to the already endless list of the rules of etiquette that I must memorize and follow. Today she explained how important it is that I never be seen without gloves. I laughed, which was a grave error, as Mama did not at all appreciate the humor. I promised I would never, ever, expose my hands, which satisfied her, at least until tomorrow's addition.

Friday, October 21, 1853

A courier comes every day to bring the Emperor dispatches and bulletins containing the most worrisome problems for his immediate consideration.

Saturday, October 22, 1853

The Emperor is gone.

He departed yesterday for Vienna, where there are affairs of state he must attend to. (It was those horrible bulletins.)

I can barely leave my room. I have cried so much since he left that my face is swollen and I cannot allow anyone to see me.

I am too despondent even to write in my diary.

Sunday, October 30, 1853

The official announcement of our engagement has appeared in the newspaper:

> His Imperial and Royal Apostolic Highness, our most gracious Lord and Emperor, Franz Joseph I, during His Majesty's stay in Bad Ischl, offered his hand to Her Most Serene Highness, Princess Elisabeth Amalie Eugenie, Duchess of Bavaria, daughter of Their Royal Highness Duke Maximilian Joseph and Duchess Ludovica, the Royal Princess of

Bavaria, after obtaining the approval of His Majesty, King Maximilian II of Bavaria, as well as Their Serene Highness the parents of the Princess-bride, and entered on an engagement. May the blessing of the Almighty rest on this event, so happy and joyful for the Imperial House and the Empire.

I was trembling when I read the announcement. Am I marrying a man or a God? I find the man so charming and admirable, but the God daunting and, by necessity, distant.

Tuesday, November 8, 1853

I have tutors who are trying to teach me French and Italian even though Mama well knows I have <u>absolutely</u> no faculty for learning a foreign language. And those aren't the only tutors I have.

I also have Count Májlath who is assigned to teach me my most important subject: the <u>entire</u> history of the empire of which I am to become Empress. He is quite competent and very imaginative — he really makes history come alive. The lessons are often so entertaining that sometimes Gackel, Néné, and Mama join us. (Néné seems to be slowly returning to her old self.)

Friday, November 11, 1853

I wish they would make up their minds. First I hear what a pleasure it is to fit me because I have such a miraculously slender figure (which is true), then I hear how difficult it is because I am so impatient, uncooperative, and fidgety (which is also true).

They want me to be available to them at the drop of a pin cushion and then, even when I do submit, they insist on taking all day for a job that should be done in a matter of minutes.

Assembling this trousseau has resulted in having seamstresses, embroiderers, milliners, and shoemakers running about all day and night.

Mama would like to postpone the wedding. She would rather we were married in June — not April — because most of Viennese society will have left the city for the summer by then and there would be less pressure on me. Mama views the Viennese court as something to be feared. She would also like the wedding to be here in Bavaria, because it would be much more convenient for us. It is quite an undertaking assembling everyone in our royal court to accompany me to Vienna.

Alas, as Mama well knows, the Archduchess would never consider either of these ideas.

In April we go to Vienna.

Saturday, November 19, 1853

Today is my name day, the feast day of St. Elisabeth, and an extraordinary diamond brooch arrived as a most elegant and timely present from the Emperor.

Friday, November 25, 1853

Mama is concerned with assembling my trousseau. I fear she is going to become the first woman in all of Bavaria to expire from overshopping. I asked her today if there was anything left for the other inhabitants of our country to purchase.

She is worried because the Viennese court is so formal. They are so inordinately concerned with appearances, she fears there is too little in my trousseau and it will be an embarrassment. Frankly, I don't know what to think.

Thursday, December 1, 1853

Hearing anyone in the family making plans for the future — a trip, an upcoming event, a joyous occasion — and knowing that it will not include me causes me so much distress that I am nearly overcome.

Wednesday, December 7, 1853

Marie is overjoyed at the prospect of moving into my room and I am not leaving for <u>months</u>.

When I heard this I couldn't help but burst into tears right in front of her. She looked so terribly confused.

Wasn't I happy that I was going to marry the Emperor and become the Empress, she asked, making me feel about two inches tall.

I told her I was happy, and then she said that if I were happy why wasn't I smiling instead of crying. The innocence of her question was enough to make me smile, briefly, through my tears.

I told her I <u>was</u> happy and I <u>wasn't</u> happy, which is the plain, simple, sad truth of it all. Moved by my own utterance and despite my most strenuous efforts, tears once again started flowing, frightening Marie and causing her to run off like a startled deer.

I went to find her so I could tell her how much I dearly and truly loved the Emperor and that falling deeply in love was a wonderful, breathtaking experience. But for me, it was also a terrifying experience because of all the duties and responsibilities I would be assuming as Empress.

I wanted to tell her that although I loved the Emperor with all my heart, I feared I was not only marrying a man but a country as well. I wanted to tell her all of this so she would understand why I was crying but she was nowhere to be found.

Wednesday, December 14, 1853

I wrote a long, heartfelt letter to Aunt Sophie wishing her the happiest of Christmases and thanking her most profusely for all that she has done for me. I confessed unashamedly that I have come to rely on her maternal affection and that I am looking forward to fulfilling my role as a dutiful and devoted daughter-in-law.

Friday, December 16, 1853

I am being painted by three separate artists and the best portrait will be chosen as a gift for the Emperor.

Mama commented today, quite out of the blue, that she thinks the Emperor is decidedly level-headed, which will be a nice counterbalance to my dreamy nature.

I wanted to tell Mama that perhaps my dreamy nature (as she calls it) will be a nice counterbalance to the Emperor's level-headedness but, on second thought, I let her remark pass without response.

Thursday, December 22, 1853

The Emperor arrived after midnight but insisted I be roused from my sleep so that he might see me without delay.

We spent the <u>entire</u> day together, which made me very happy.

He brought with him a traveling breakfast service with an E and the imperial crown engraved on it and a bouquet of fresh roses from the Archduchess. He said that when I am the Empress I shall have fresh roses all year round — even in the winter.

Sunday, December 25, 1853

I have a bad cold, which is ruining my birthday and Christmas celebration, although I am buoyed by the Emperor's most solicitous nature. He said he wished there was something he could do that would prevent me from ever having a cold for as long as I lived.

Last night on horseback, we exchanged portraits of each other. In addition, the Emperor gave me three parrots from the menagerie in the Schönbrunn Palace, which are more precious than all the jewels I have received thus far.

Unfortunately, matters of state once again forced the Emperor to return precipitously to Vienna. His duties plague him twenty-four hours a day, seven days a week, and exhaust almost all of his time.

Tuesday, January 3, 1854

My trousseau is nearly complete:
  1 blue velvet cloak (the one with the sable trim and muff that the Emperor gave me)
  4 ball gowns (2 white, 1 pink, 1 sky blue with white roses)
17 formal gowns with trains
  1 wedding dress (with silver moiré overdress)
  1 black mourning gown (for court mourning)
19 thin summer dresses (rose, violet, forget-me-not blue)
  4 low-cut ballroom crinolines
  4 corsets
  3 riding corsets
  6 cloaks

8 lighter, sleeveless cloaks

5 velvet capelets

16 hats with feathers, roses, violets, wildflowers, and veils

6 dressing gowns

11 embroidered nightcaps

3 negligé caps of embroidered muslin

24 neckerchiefs

24 combing coats

3 bathing shirts

19 dozen chemises of batiste and lace

14 dozen pairs of stockings of silk, cotton, and wool

6 dozen petticoats of piqué, silk, and flannel

5 dozen pantalets

1 dozen bed jackets

113 pairs of shoes (Mama says I will simply have to obtain more once I get to Vienna because, as Empress, I am forbidden to wear shoes more than once and must, at the end of the day, give them away.)

Miscellaneous: 2 fans; 2 umbrellas; 3 large parasols; 3 small parasols; tortoiseshell combs, clothes brushes, hairbrushes, nailbrushes, toothbrushes, shoehorns, hairpins, straight pins, ribbons, and buttons.

Sunday, January 22, 1854

I am so busy with all the preparations for the wedding I no longer even have time each day to record that day's events in my diary.

Sunday, January 29, 1854

I didn't realize until now how precious my family is to me. Now I know I love them even more than I thought. I can't imagine saying good-bye to everyone.

Wednesday, February 15, 1854

Everything I see at Possi reminds me that soon it will no longer be my home. My cozy bed will not be mine and my desk will be used by someone other than me.

I stare at my ink-stained writing table for hours and hours. I can remember each and every stain: what I was thinking, the poem I was writing, or the diary entry I was making.

Knowing I will never sit at my desk again caused a shudder to run through my body.

Friday, February 24, 1854

I never liked saying good-bye to anything I love. Not to Poppy, not to Punch, or any of my precious pets. Now I have to leave and say good-bye to all of them at once.

Saturday, February 25, 1854

Mama is upset because I am going to be leaving her for-ever. I assured her that I am not leaving her <u>forever</u>, but I fear beneath it all she is right. I feel like I am about to step from my childhood to the world of an Empress without a moment to catch my breath or any time to buffer the impact.

Wednesday, March 1, 1854

Count Májlath has been concentrating on Hungarian history, which he is quite passionate about. The Count's portrayal of his people's desire for independence is a poignant one. And I was happy to learn that, like me, they have a great love of horses.

Tuesday, March 14, 1854

The Emperor arrived today bearing the opal-and-diamond tiara and matching necklace that Aunt Sophie wore to her wedding. They are the most magnificent objects I have ever, ever beheld. The Emperor urged Mama to make sure the set is put immediately in a safe place.

The day was ruined, unfortunately, by the Emperor's most unexpected rebuke that I was entirely too familiar in the way I addressed his mother in my most recent letter.

He said I must be sure to be more respectful in my choice of salutations and more careful in my tone of voice. He was rather harsh at the outset and needless to say, I was stunned by this most unanticipated speech. Sensing that I was recoiling from this unpleasant remonstrance, he spent some time patiently explaining that the Archduchess's attitude was nothing more than the feeling of austerity and authority that occurs to someone of her age and position.

To me this was all just a lot of words.

No matter what I do Aunt Sophie seems to find some way to find fault with me. For the longest time I have been pretending that this isn't so, but now it is undeniable. Even back in August when we were in Ischl, she was constantly looking at me with the most penetrating gaze, as if she mightily disapproved of her son's choice.

There was the matter of my yellow teeth and telling Mama that something had to be done about them before the wedding. Then there was the complaint that I was riding too much and now this.

And we're not even married yet!

I can't imagine what's next but I am afraid I will find out sooner than I would like.

I was only trying to act as I thought a proper future daughter-in-law should but I can now see that that was a most misguided approach. I assured the Emperor that it would not happen again, and I would, as he requested, refer to her forever and always as "Beloved and Honored Archduchess."

I don't understand what he wants of me sometimes. I know he loves me for my willfulness and impetuousness (he's as much as told me so), but at the same time he wants me to be dutiful and obedient.

Tuesday, March 21, 1854

A letter from the Emperor.

He complimented me on all the new things I am learning and said how very proud I am going to make him.

Saturday, April 1, 1854

In twenty-four days I shall be married!

Thursday, April 6, 1854

All sorts of uncontrollable thoughts race through my mind as my wedding approaches. I merely fly from one to the other, never stopping long enough at any one, like a honeybee busily visiting each flower in an endless field of wildflowers.

Friday, April 7, 1854

As if I didn't feel bad enough already, now I find out that all the little ones are not coming with us to the wedding because Mama thinks that the journey will be too long and the circumstances and ceremony surrounding the royal wedding too much of a strain on them.

Thursday, April 13, 1854

Mama has declared that everything seems to be in order (at last). There are seventeen large trunks and eight smaller ones, each filled to overflowing and now ready to be sent on ahead with the servants.

Saturday, April 15, 1854
Munich, Bavaria

The whole family is gathered here for a final farewell. I wore the Archduchess's diamonds, which were most impressive.

I had gifts prepared for the gardener and his wife, the forester, the boatman, the grooms, and all of the house servants. I will miss them terribly.

Tuesday, April 18, 1854
Possenhofen, Bavaria

I leave in two days.

I must say good-bye to my childhood.

> Though again you greet the May,
>   Now farewell, beloved castle —
> I shall be so far away!

I leave tomorrow for Vienna, to marry the Emperor and become the Empress of Austria.

> O swallow, thy swift pinions lend me,
>   And be my guide to lands afar,
> Happy to break the toils that bind me
>   And shatter every prison bar.
>
> Oh, could I but with thee be fleeing
>   Through the blue eternities of sky,
> How I would praise with all my being
>   The God, whom men call Liberty.
>
> How soon would I forget all sorrow,
>   Forget the old love and the new,
> And never fear a sad tomorrow
>   Never let the tears my cheeks bedew.

Friday, April 21, 1854
Linz, Austria

A most unexpected and pleasant surprise awaited me upon our arrival late this afternoon in Linz: The Emperor was there to greet me! We have not seen each other in such a long time — four weeks — that I had nearly forgotten how handsome he is. He wanted to be certain that I was escorted safely to our lodgings. Sometimes I marvel at the extent of the Emperor's consideration. Imagine traveling all the way from Vienna, just to make sure I am properly settled.

It is most unfortunate that he has to return to Vienna before me (at daybreak) to see that everything is proceeding as planned.

All of Vienna is busy preparing for the royal wedding, and everyone is praying for fair weather. My picture is displayed in the windows of every shop and coffeehouse and little porcelain figures of the two of us on horseback are being collected by the people. The Emperor delighted in telling me that excitement is at such a fevered pitch that no one talks about anything else, not even the war. (This was the first I have heard that there is a war somewhere.)

He assured me that the people of Vienna already love me because they know how happy I have made him. This is a lovely sentiment but one which I can hardly believe.

Later this evening we are all going to the theater to see a performance of *The Roses of Elisabeth*, which will be followed by a torchlight parade.

Seeing the Emperor helped take my mind off the sadness of saying good-bye to Gackel at Straubing from whence he returned home to Bavaria. Mama promised he could visit me this summer but I am not sure if she really means it or if she was just saying it to make our parting less painful. I am much relieved that Mama will remain by my side throughout our journey.

Saturday, April 22, 1854
Vienna, Austria

We departed from Linz early this morning aboard the most magnificent side-wheeler aptly named the *Franz Joseph*. Our cabin was covered in crimson velvet, and there was a garden and a rose arbor on deck. The sides of the ship were decorated with roses and the blue-and-white flags of Bavaria flew side by side with the yellow-and-black Habsburg banners. No other vessels were permitted on the Danube so we flowed down undisturbed all the way to Nussdorf.

Hundreds of deliriously happy, cheering people — men, women, and children — lined the banks, all of them shouting my name. I did not know quite what to do so I just smiled and waved to them with my lace handkerchief, which only made them cheer all the more.

At each landing, we met groups of local dignitaries and listened to addresses, proclamations, and speeches while the imperial anthem was played and bursts of cannon fire sounded in the background.

Before arriving at Nussdorf, I removed my traveling outfit and put on my nice pink dress with the full crinoline, a white lace cape, and a small white cap.

At Nussdorf, the Emperor was there once again to meet me. I was most embarrassed by his uncharacteristically impetuous behavior: leaping onto the boat even <u>before</u> it had safely docked and taking me into his arms and kissing me perhaps a little too arduously for public consumption. Not only was his family there, and I can't even say how many public officials, but also thousands and thousands of spectators whose sole purpose was to watch us.

The Emperor most gallantly offered me his arm, which I eagerly took as I was already feeling fatigued from the journey and unnerved by the excitement and constant attention.

He led me to the Imperial carriage, which took us to Schönbrunn, where still more people were waiting to greet us. The Imperial Palace was as astonishing as Mama said it would be. When she told me there were fourteen hundred and forty-one rooms, I didn't believe her. But now that I have seen it I do. The hundreds and hundreds of windows all seemed to be peering down, judging and scrutinizing me, much as Aunt Sophie does.

There were royal ladies and gentlemen standing shoulder to shoulder in the gardens and wall to wall inside: on top of the stairs, on each stair, and all along the Gallery of Mirrors.

Aunt Sophie introduced me to the other Archduchesses and the Emperor introduced me to their male counterparts. I whispered to the Emperor — I could see that we were not to be left alone — that I was uncertain how to greet each distinguished guest, which was causing me a great amount of distress. He said that in time it will all become second nature to me, as it had to him. Apparently, that put the matter to rest for him but, unfortunately, "in time" did me little good right now, and my concerns still lingered most troublingly.

I proceeded as best I could to greet everyone, accepting their gifts most graciously, murmuring my most heartfelt thanks, and earnestly assuring them that their gift was the <u>most</u> beautiful of all, even though I was so tired I couldn't tell a gift from a bowl of soup.

I was so delighted when I saw the only familiar faces in the crowd — Cousin Abelgunde and Cousin Hildegarde from Bavaria — that when they approached, I hugged them as I had done all my life.

In an instant, I could feel everyone's disapproval. One furtive glance confirmed my feelings. They looked outraged, as if I had committed some wholly unacceptable breach of conduct, which it turns out I had.

The Archduchess pulled me aside at once and advised me in the most stern manner that proper protocol must be observed and that hugging even one's cousins was simply not done by someone of my exalted position and that they, like every other soul in the empire, must kiss my hand.

Although the Emperor could see that I was distraught from this encounter, and so disturbed as to be in need of immediate rest, he explained that I was obligated to proceed onto the main balcony and wave to the multitudes gathered below.

I was so unsure and unsteady I had to hold on to the stone railing. Beneath me was a sea of people all shouting my name, <u>Elisabeth, Elisabeth, Elisabeth</u>, over and over and over.

Back inside there were still more people to meet and greet. I was introduced to the Mistress of the Robes, Countess Esztherházy, who was even older than Mama and reminded me, in spirit if not body, of Baroness Wulfen, and toward whom I took an instant dislike (which appeared to be quite mutual). The Countess introduced me to two younger ladies-in-waiting who seemed much more pleasant.

The Countess Esztherházy, who is mistress of my private household, said she would guide me through all the court duties and ceremonies I would be required to follow.

She stressed that it was of the utmost importance that everything proceed efficiently.

She explained that my household would consist of a secretary, a lady of the bedchamber, two lady's maids, two chambermaids, one valet de chambre, a porter, four footmen, and one houseman.

All I could think of was sleep but I could see that it was not to be, not soon, anyway.

Finally, the Countess bid me good night but not before handing me the "Order for the Ceremonial and Public Entry into Vienna of her Royal Highness and Most Austere Princess Elisabeth," saying, as she left that I should be sure to memorize every line by morning.

I have so much to do that I don't know what to do first.

Sunday, April 23, 1854

I don't think I really slept <u>at all</u> last night. When I awoke this morning, I was just as tired as when I laid my head down. I don't know which was worse, having the soldiers standing guard outside my door or wondering if they were keeping someone out or me in.

After spending countless hours getting dressed this morning, we traveled to the ancient Imperial castle where we had to wait for the state carriage that was to take me on a circuit of Vienna for everyone to see.

All I seem to do since I left Bavaria is meet people I don't know, wave to crowds of screaming people, and go from one vehicle to the next in rapid succession.

By the time we entered the state carriage, it was already late in the afternoon. I dreaded going in that carriage. I cried and told Mama I felt like someone in a circus sideshow. Mama frowned and reminded me of my duties to the people of Vienna.

The carriage was simply from another world: all glass and gold with brilliantly painted panels. It was drawn by four pairs of the most magnificent, snow-white Lipizzaner horses, their manes plaited with red-and-gold tassels with white plumes sprouting skyward and their harnesses adorned with emeralds and gold.

We were escorted by two white-wigged footmen wearing three-cornered hats, trumpeters, postilions and outriders dressed in gold and black, and pages and chamberlains in scarlet and white.

There were dignitaries in front of us and dignitaries

behind us. We composed quite a long procession and we proceeded at a snail's pace.

Pretty girls dressed all in white tossed rose petals in our path.

The houses were decorated with bunting and flowers and the people were standing on a specially built platform. As we neared the city walls church bells began to peal.

The streets were overflowing with people who leaned against the soldiers and police who did their best to contain them. Despite the officers' best efforts, the crowd broke through from time to time, attempting to get a closer look at me, the captured animal that was being displayed both for her exotic nature and so that all could see that she had finally been tamed and was now safely confined to a glass cage.

"Long live the Empress," they shouted again and again.

When we arrived at the Hofburg Palace in the center of Vienna, the Emperor was waiting to greet me at the threshold. Unfortunately upon leaving the carriage, I struck the diamond tiara I was wearing on the door frame, having completely forgotten that I was wearing it. Miraculously I caught it and was able to resettle it without any further damage to it or my delicate state of mind.

The Hofburg was as dismal and gloomy as Schönbrunn although not nearly as overwhelmingly large. Most appalling, like Schönbrunn, there was not one bathroom to be found in the entire place. No bathrooms, no lavatories, and no running water of <u>any kind</u>, which was quite a shock. They still use chamber pots and carry them down those long, echoing corridors where anyone and everyone can see everything.

The thought of living my life there sends shivers down my spine.

Monday, April 24, 1854

The very first thing that greeted me at seven o'clock on this, the morning of my wedding day, was Countess Esztherházy bearing two more of those huge, thick manuscripts for my immediate consumption.

One, humorously titled "Most Humble Reminders," explained in exquisite nineteen-page detail every aspect of the wedding ceremony that was now only twelve hours away. When I was to bow, when I was to open my mouth, and what was to come out. What, in fact, I was to do at <u>each</u> and <u>every</u> second of the ceremony.

The Countess said that the Archduchess wanted me to be sure to memorize all of this at the earliest possible moment.

The second listed each and every member of the royal court, their relative rank, who could enter my apartment without knocking (they were called "admissible persons"), and who had to wait (like ladies-in-waiting) divided into "little waits" and "big waits."

Although the parish church was mercifully close — only fifty yards away — it still took us an hour to wend our way through the tortuous courtyards and corridors of the palace. The crowds were so thick, the streets had to be closed so we could proceed.

The Emperor rode alone at the head of the procession looking, as always, regal and commanding in his field marshal's uniform. I thanked the heavens that my wedding dress was as beautiful as I hoped and prayed it would be. The white silk embroidered with gold and silver thread was, as Mama assured me it would be, <u>perfect</u>. Mama also said my hair looked splendid, although I was distracted by how suddenly oppressive and heavy Aunt Sophie's tiara felt.

Thousands of candles inside the church created an other-worldly glow, illuminating the presence of more prelates, envoys, men in uniform, royal ladies, and dignitaries from every corner of the Empire and most of the countries of Europe.

Accompanied by Mama and Aunt Sophie, I advanced down the aisle looking neither right nor left, afraid of what I might see there. I could feel the silence that fell all around me as we entered and was painfully aware of the color leaving my face with such speed that I was certain I was going to collapse at any moment.

I hesitated before approaching the high altar and the Emperor touched my arm as if to remind me what I was to do. This was most timely and appropriate for I had already entered a netherworld somewhere between the real and the not real, where everything is just a little less clear, a little less certain.

I head a faint voice in the distance, or was it? It was asking me a question. "Yes," I said, knowing that was the right answer, the answer everyone — Mama, Aunt Sophie, the Emperor, and all the people of Vienna — was waiting to hear.

I was certain I barely spoke above a whisper but as soon as the word left my lips it seemed to take flight, lofting up to the ceiling and increasing in volume as if the Lord himself were affirming my affirmation.

We were kneeling and the Emperor held my trembling hand in his and placed the band of gold on my finger. There was the sound of artillery being fired and the church bells pealing, somewhere.

The Archbishop of Vienna spoke and spoke and spoke. His incomprehensible oratory was so tedious that I wanted to scream out, "Oh stop, please stop, I will do anything if you just stop!" Somehow I managed to hold my tongue as he droned on and on, speech ceasing to be speech, sentences reduced merely to words without meaning: nobility, bond, harmony, honor, purity, duty, devotion.

I remember being back at the palace but I don't remember how I got there.

There was one obligatory ceremonial function followed by another. I remember seeing Mama and Aunt Sophie in tears, Karl Ludwig looking forlorn, and Néné looking happy and hoping she was. I remember the Emperor sitting next to me on the royal throne, people bowing, kissing my hand, and offering me their congratulations. And I remember not uttering a single word.

Each time I entered a room everyone would burst into applause and all I could think was how curious that all this was happening to me.

I remember being too tired to eat supper. Aunt Sophie and Mama took me to my room while twelve pages carried golden candelabra leading and lighting the way down the twisted corridors as the wind shook the shutters.

I remember wanting to be alone with Mama but knowing that that was not to be; Countess Esztherházy and the maids preparing my bedchamber, assisting me with my dressing and grooming, waiting while I said my prayers.

I was so relieved when they left.

At last I could be alone to record this, the most important day of my life, in my most precious diary.

Now, as I write, I have only to await the Emperor's knock.

Epilogue

The Emperor and his Princess Bride did not live happily ever after.

While still on her honeymoon Elisabeth wrote:

> Oh, had I but never left the path
> That would have led me to freedom.
> Oh, that on the broad avenues
> Of vanity I had never strayed!
>
> I have awakened in a dungeon,
> With chains on my hands.
> And my longing ever stronger —
> And freedom!
> You, turned from me!

I have awakened from a rapture,
Which held my spirit captive,
And vainly do I curse this exchange,
In which I gambled away you — freedom — away.

She would spend the rest of her life struggling to rid herself of those chains and to regain her freedom.

Her imperious mother-in-law intended to remain the power behind the throne. She watched Elisabeth's every move, constantly finding fault and dominating her at every turn. She took over the raising of Elisabeth's first two children: hiring the nursemaids, insisting that the nursery be near her, and making it impossible for Sisi to be alone with her children. Elisabeth did not even participate in the naming of her first born, Sophie (after her grandmother). Sisi's relationship with her mother-in-law grew more strained over time.

Meanwhile, the Emperor remained silent. The obedient son was unable or unwilling to defend or protect his sixteen-year-old bride. The Emperor and Elisabeth were rarely alone. Every meal was eaten with the royal family and the appropriate attendants. At dinner, the Emperor hardly ever spoke and therefore no one else did. When he was done, the dishes were cleared and the meal was officially over.

Their marriage became distant and strained. Elisabeth once wrote, "I cannot understand how people can look forward to marriage so much and expect so much good to result from it. It is a ridiculous institution. . . . I think of myself, sold as a child of fifteen and taking an oath I did not understand and could never undo."

Her dislike and disapproval of the rigidity and extreme formality of the Viennese court was apparent to all. She balked at every turn: eating without gloves, unlike the rest of the royal family, refusing to discard her shoes after each wearing, and, shockingly, resuming riding only a month after giving birth.

Only too late did the Emperor realize that Sisi was a poor choice to play the role of devoted wife and dutiful Empress.

Abandoned and alone, surrounded by strangers who wished her ill and gossiped behind her back, she spent endless hours sobbing in her room. As she did when she was a child of ten, she turned to writing poetry, hoping it would alleviate her sadness.

Strong-willed and defiant by nature, Elisabeth became

more self-confident. By the time she was twenty-eight she was determined to raise her fourth child by herself. She wrote to her no-doubt stunned husband:

"I wish to have reserved to me the absolute authority in all matters concerning the children, the choice of the people around them, the place of their residence, the complete supervision of their education, in a word, everything is to be left entirely to me to decide, until the moment of their majority. I further wish that, whatever concerns my personal affairs, such as, among others, the choice of the people around me, the places of my residence, all arrangements in the house, etc., be reserved to me alone to decide."

Although the Emperor never spoke to her of such lofty matters as world politics she became a keen student on her own.

She formed liberal ideas, preferring a republic to a monarchy, kingdom, or empire — a view understandably not shared by the Emperor or his mother.

She studied Austrian history, especially the literature and history of Hungary. Her rebellious nature identified with the Hungarian desire for independence. She learned to speak their language (as well as reading and speaking in eight other modern languages and classical Latin and Greek).

A truly caring person, she developed a sincere concern for the poor and mentally ill. She became a symbol of hope to hundreds of thousands of her subjects.

But it was Elisabeth's extraordinary beauty that was her most noteworthy characteristic. And the crowning glory of her beauty was her magnificent, floor-length, auburn hair.

It took three hours each day to fix it properly. Washing it in the cognac and egg mixture she preferred could take the entire day. Maintaining it required artistry, craftsmanship and, at times, guile.

Nothing less than magic would do.

Knowing that the Empress would be in a frenzy if even one strand of hair fell out, her hairdresser stuck stray hairs on a piece of adhesive she hid under the hem of her apron.

There were no bad-hair days for Elisabeth. If her favorite hairdresser was sick she simply would not come out of her bedroom. "I am a slave to my hair," she said.

Elisabeth was five-foot-seven and a half inches tall

(taller than the Emperor, although paintings show him taller), with an astonishing twenty-inch waist made even tinier by tight lacing. (Sometimes Elisabeth had herself sewn right into her clothing.)

She was the reigning beauty of her day.

What she wore, how she fixed her hair, and what she looked like was daily grist for the media and gossip stream of the times.

Even her defects contributed to the legend. Self-conscious about her teeth, she parted her lips reluctantly and as little as possible. She spoke in a whisper that was barely audible, adding to the mystery that surrounded her.

She had a gymnasium built that included dumbbells, parallel bars, rings, and ropes hung from the ceiling. She fenced, hiked great distances, and "power-walked" for hours over various terrains in all kinds of weather (tiring out one lady-in-waiting after another).

And of course, Elisabeth rode horses. In her day, she was a better rider than any woman and most men. Her communication with her mounts was known to be telepathic.

She weighed herself three times a day. Sisi devoted endless hours caring for her skin via a variety of facial masks. A silk one to eliminate freckles and two others consisting of raw veal and crushed strawberries. She took a cold bath every morning, hot oil baths, and special massages periodically, and slept with hot towels tied to her waist. Her beauty became an obsession that led to one exotic starvation diet after another and, eventually, what we would now recognize as anorexia nervosa.

Predictably, her mental and physical health faltered. Seeking relief, presumably in better climates, she traveled all over the world (with forty tons of luggage and ninety attendants) accompanied by her beloved Newfoundlands, Saint Bernards, and Great Danes.

She was gone for longer and longer periods of time, preferring, it appeared, to be anywhere but Vienna. The Emperor and the Empress saw each other rarely and led virtually separate lives. Never-ending movement appeared to be the solution she had chosen for her unhappy life.

Aging terrified her. She hid her face behind a fan or a parasol and refused to be photographed or sketched. There are no pictures of her in later life.

"As soon as I feel myself aging, I shall retire from the world altogether. There is nothing more 'horrendous' than gradually becoming mummified and unwilling to say farewell to youth. To go around as a rouged larva —

dreadful! Perhaps later, I shall always wear a veil, and even those close to me will no longer see my face."

The death of her son Rudolf — a victim of a double suicide with his mistress — was a crushing blow from which she never fully recovered.

In September 1898, while traveling in Geneva, Switzerland, a political extremist stabbed her to death with a rusty file he had fashioned with a wooden handle into a dagger.

She was sixty.

Life in Austria

Historical Note

A legendary beauty who rebelled against the strict rituals and suffocating privileges of her title, Empress Elisabeth's life often reflected the tumultuous times in which she lived.

In 1848, five years before the Emperor Franz Joseph set eyes on Elisabeth, Europe was seized by a series of revolutions. In that one year, the ruling powers of France, Germany, Austria, and Italy were all overthrown. However, in each case the uprisings were quickly suppressed, mostly because the upstarts were poorly organized and could not agree on a clear set of goals. But, even in failure, the revolutions of 1848 set into motion the changes that would shape the twentieth century.

That same year also saw the publication of the *Communist Manifesto* by Karl Marx and Friedrich Engels. This classic work memorably expressed many of the issues raised by the failed revolutions, particularly aspects concerned with the conditions of the working classes. Of course, Marx and Engels would not have had to fight for the working classes if a far different kind of revolution hadn't already been in progress — namely, the Industrial Revolution.

The Industrial Revolution began in seventeenth-century Great Britain and became a worldwide phenomenon between 1860 and 1890. (Elisabeth became Empress in 1854 and remained in the public eye until she was fatally stabbed in 1898.) It was a period during which the world shifted from societies based on farming and simple tools to societies that relied on complex machines to manufacture goods. The first such machine to set the Industrial Revolution in motion was the steam engine, invented in 1705 by Englishman Thomas Newcomen and improved by James Watt in 1763. Soon after came the railroads, the telegraph, and electric power.

During Elisabeth's lifetime, each day promised new miracles of invention, innovation, and discovery. In 1852, Elisha Graves Otis invented the elevator brake in Yonkers, New York, which made towering, multi-story skyscrapers a

practical reality. Previously there was no way to lift eleva-
tors up and down dozens of floors without endangering
passengers. Then, in 1859, the English naturalist Charles
Darwin published *On the Origin of Species,* which introduced the notion of evolution through natural selection,
creating a never-ending debate about man's place in the
animal kingdom. In the years following Darwin's findings,
the French scientist Louis Pasteur discovered the process
(named pasteurization after him) that kills disease-causing
organisms in milk, orange juice, beer, and other liquids,
making them safer to drink. And showing the range of
discovery in this period, in 1866 Swedish engineer Alfred
Nobel invented dynamite, which would bring a new level
of violence to the face of war. Ironically, the fortune he
amassed from this and other inventions would eventually
allow for the creation of the Nobel Peace Prize.

In 1848, while Europe weathered constant upheaval
and turmoil, droves of Americans headed west to cash
in on the California Gold Rush. One such person was
twenty-year-old Levi Strauss, who began making durable
trousers out of canvas for miners, who tended to quickly
wear through their pants. Eventually, in 1873, Levi
patented what had become his own personal gold mine,

christening it the "blue jean." Other inventions included the telephone by Alexander Graham Bell in 1876 and the lightbulb by Thomas Edison in 1879. In 1886, John S. Pemberton created what would eventually become one of the world's most recognizable symbols: Coca-Cola. One invention that Elisabeth, who was known to sew herself into her clothes, would have undoubtedly appreciated (had she lived long enough) was the zipper, invented by Whitcomb L. Judson and patented in 1893.

But not all products of the Industrial Revolution were for the good of mankind. Some of the more odious consequences of industrialization were child labor and terrible working conditions. Long hours for low wages in cramped spaces where safety was at best an afterthought all contributed to some of the unrest and sense of inequality that lead to the revolutions of 1848. On the other hand, though they hardly fared better than men in the workforce, the ability of women to earn their own wages would lead to greater demands for female independence and equality — motivations that would not have been unfamiliar to Elisabeth. But in the end, the deplorable working conditions of the times did not go unnoticed, and popular novels such as *Hard Times* by Charles Dickens, *Mary*

Barton by Elizabeth Gaskell, and later, *The Jungle* by Upton Sinclair helped better the plight of the working classes around the world.

But there was no better example of the transformations shaping the world during Elisabeth's lifetime than those experienced by the vast empire over which she and her husband ruled. When Elisabeth was plucked from her idyllic, small-town life in Bavaria to become the Empress of Austria, she became a member of one of the world's oldest ruling families.

The Habsburg dynasty ruled Austria and its surrounding lands from 1282 until the end of World War I in 1918. By the time Elisabeth entered royal life, the storied history of the Habsburgs was already in steep decline. With its empire stretched thin, and increasingly at odds with the various nations under its crown, the 1848 revolution in Austria led to the abdication of Emperor Ferdinand I, who was then replaced by his more popular, eighteen-year-old nephew, Franz Joseph.

Yet as revered and idolized as he was, the new Emperor was no match for the onward march of history. During Franz Joseph's reign, Austria lost its dominance in both Italy in 1859 and Germany in 1866. (On the other side of the globe, America endured its own turmoil as it suffered through a costly civil war.) Then in 1867, partly due to Elisabeth's Hungarian sympathies, the Habsburg lands were reorganized into the Austro-Hungarian empire, with a dual monarchy at the head of the Austrian (Habsburg) Empire and the Kingdom of Hungary. These were momentous events that signaled the eventual rise of nation-states governed by elected officials rather than dynastic governance by individuals born into power. Monarchs, where they remained, shared power with secular leaders and representatives; many were left with only symbolic power.

The Austro-Hungarian monarchy limped on, with its luster dimmed with the murder of Empress Elisabeth in 1898. But signs of the world to come could already be seen in its capital city, Vienna, one of the world's first modern urban centers. In 1857, its ancient city walls were destroyed and replaced by grand boulevards, imposing buildings, and public parks. It was here that psychoanalyst Sigmund Freud discovered the mysteries of the mind, and composers like Johannes Brahms, Gustav Mahler, and Arnold Schoenberg forever altered the sound of music. Painters like Gustav Klimt and Egon Schiele visualized the spirit of the times in their controversial works. More than any other city in the world, Empress Elisabeth's Vienna represented the new world looming ahead.

In 1914, the man who was to be Franz Joseph's heir to the Austro-Hungarian throne, the Archduke Francis Ferdinand, was assassinated along with his wife, in the name of Serbian independence. This single act would set off World War I, the deadliest war the world until then had ever seen, and the end of which would bring about the total collapse of Habsburg rule.

Maximilian I Joseph
King of Bavaria
(1756–1825)
r. 1806–1825
= Karoline Baden

Ladovica
(1808–1892)
=
Maximilian Joseph
Duke in Bavaria
(1808–1888)

Franz Karl
(1802–1878)
=
Sophie
(1805–1920)

Karl Ludwig
(1833–1896)
(1) Margaret
=
(2) Annunziata
=
(3) Marie
Theresia

Max Emmanuel
(1849–1893)
=
Amelie of
Saxe-Coburg

Marie
(1841–1925)
=
Francisco II
King of the
Two Sicilies

Sophie
(1847–1897)
=
Ferdinand
Duke of Alençon

Ferdinand Max
Emperor of Mexico
(1832–1867)
=
Carlotta

Karl Theodor
(1839–1909)
=
(1) Sophie
of Saxony
(1845–1867)
=
(2) Marie José
of Braganza
(1847–1943)

Henriette
Mendel
=
Ludwig
(1831–1920)

Helene
(1834–1890)
=
Maximillian
Prince of Thurn
and Taxis

Prince Lodovico
of the Two Sicilies
=
Mathilde
(1843–1925)

Elisabeth (Sisi)
(1837–1898)
Empress of Austria (r. 1854–1916)
Queen of Hungary (r. 1867–1898)

Franz Joseph I
(1830–1916)
Emperor of Austria (r. 1848–1916)
King of Hungary (r. 1867–1916)

Gisela
(1856–1932)
=
Leopold of
Bavaria

Rudolph
(1858–1889)
=
Stephanie
of Belgium

Marie Valerie
(1868–1924)
=
Franz Salvator

Sophie
(1855–1857)

The Wittelsbach-Habsburg Family Tree

The marriage of Elisabeth, Princess of Bavaria, to Archduke Franz Joseph I, Emperor of Austria and Prince Royal (later, King) of Hungary, formed yet another link between the Wittelsbach rulers of Bavaria and the Habsburg Dynasty (heirs since 1438 to the crown lands of Germany and the Holy Roman Empire). In the eighteenth and nineteenth centuries, the House of Wittelsbach successfully used marriages to enhance the family's fortunes and to maneuver between Prussia and Austria, the powerful northern and southern rivals, for control of the German empire. Historically, the imperial Habsburg Dynasty was one of the greatest and most influential of Europe's royal houses. Franz Joseph I proved to be the last important Habsburg emperor, as Prussia rose to power and the age of great princes in Europe came to a close.

The family tree chart portrays the familial connections between Franz Joseph I and Elisabeth, beginning with their grandparents. The crown symbol indicates those who ruled nations. Double lines represent marriages; single lines indicate parentage. Dates of births and deaths (when available) are noted.

Elisabeth's Parents

Duke Maximilian Joseph: Born in 1808, Maximilian was twenty years old when he married Ludovica, Princess of Bavaria. A talented writer, he was beloved in his country for being a great patron of the arts. He died in 1888.

Duchess Ludovica (Luisa) Wilhelmina Wittelsbach, Royal Princess of Bavaria: Born in 1808 to Maximilian I Joseph Wittelsbach, King of Bavaria, she married below her station when she wed her cousin Maximilian Joseph, who was a mere duke. Together the couple had eight children. She died in 1892.

Children of Duke Maximilian Joseph and Duchess Ludovica

Ludwig: Firstborn son. In 1859, he married a young actress named Henriette Mendel, causing a scandal since the marriage followed the birth of their daughter.

Helene: Firstborn daughter. Nicknamed "Néné," she was betrothed to Emperor Franz Joseph I but was quickly passed over for her younger sister Elisabeth. Later, she married Prince Maximillian of Thurn and Taxis. The couple had four children.

Elisabeth Amelie Eugenie: Princess of Bavaria, Empress of Austria, and Queen of Hungary, nicknamed "Sisi." Born on Christmas Eve, 1837, Elisabeth was the third child of Duke Maximilian Joseph and Duchess Ludovica. Betrothed at age fifteen to Habsburg Emperor Franz Joseph I, at age sixteen she was married on April 24, 1854, to the twenty-four-year-old monarch in the Augustine Church in Vienna. Together they had four children. She died on September 10, 1898, in Geneva, Switzerland, after an Italian anarchist stabbed her to death.

Karl Theodor: Second son and Elisabeth's favorite brother. Nicknamed "Gackel," he studied medicine and became an ophthalmologist. He married twice: first to Sophie of Saxony, who died two years into the marriage, then nine years later to Marie José of Braganza. Together they had five children.

Marie: Fifth child of the duke and duchess. In 1859, she married Francisco II, who was the heir to the throne of the Two Sicilies.

Mathilde: Sixth child, nicknamed "Spatz." She married the brother of Francisco II, Lodovico. Unfortunately, the marriage was an ill-fated union, and Lodovico, who suffered from frequent nervous breakdowns, hanged himself.

Sophie: The seventh child, at twenty years old she was engaged to her cousin, King Ludwig II of Bavaria, also known as "Mad King Ludwig" or the "Swan King" because of his rumored insanity and his love of swans. Unfortunately, Ludwig was not very interested in marrying Sophie and ended the engagement. Shortly after, Sophie married the Duke of Alençon. They had two children.

Max Emmanuel: Elisabeth's youngest sibling, he was nicknamed "Mapperl." He married Princess Amelie of Saxe-Coburg, and together they had three children.

Elisabeth's Husband
Franz Joseph I: Emperor of Austria and King of Hungary. Born on August 18, 1830, in Vienna, he was the eldest son of Archduke Franz Karl and his wife, Sophie, Princess of Bavaria and Archduchess of Austria (her younger sister, Ludovica, was Elisabeth's mother). Franz Joseph was eighteen years old when his uncle Ferdinand I abdicated the throne in 1848 in favor of his nephew. Franz Joseph's rule of Austria-Hungary ended with his death on November 21, 1916, two years after World War I began with the assassination of his nephew, Prince Franz Ferdinand, in Sarajevo, Serbia.

Children of Elisabeth and Franz Joseph

Archduchess Sophie Fredericke Dorothea: Born on March 5, 1855, the infant princess was taken from her mother upon birth and given to the care of her grandmother, Archduchess Sophie, who named the child after herself. The Emperor's mother intended to raise Franz Joseph and Elisabeth's children personally. On May 29, 1857, at two years old, Sophie died of the measles while in Buda, Hungary.

Archduchess Gisela Louise Marie: Born on June 12, 1856, the Empress Elisabeth's second daughter was also raised from birth by her grandmother. Gisela married Prince Leopold of Bavaria on April 20, 1873, when she was sixteen years old. They had four children. Gisela died in Munich, the Bavarian capital, on July 27, 1932.

Crown Prince Rudolph Franz Karl Joseph: Born on August 21, 1858, he was named by his father after the first Habsburg emperor. On May 10, 1881, he married Princess Stephanie, the seventeen-year-old daughter of King Leopold II of Belgium. They had a daughter, Elisabeth Marie Henriette, on September 2, 1883. This arranged marriage was not a happy one for Rudolph, who began to show signs of serious depression. On January 30, 1889, he and his young mistress, Baroness Marie

Vetsera, were found dead, having committed suicide at Franz Joseph's hunting lodge, Mayerling.

Archduchess Marie Valerie Mathilde: Born in Buda, Hungary, on April 22, 1868, Marie Valerie was the only child the Empress Elisabeth was allowed to raise from birth herself. Marie Valerie married the Archduke Franz Salvator of Austria-Tuscany on July 31, 1890, at Bad Ischl, where her mother and father had first met. The couple had nine children together. Archduchess Marie Valerie died on September 6, 1924.

Photograph of sixteen-year-old Elisabeth in her wedding dress. She married twenty-four-year-old Emperor Franz Joseph on April 24, 1854.

Portrait of a young Franz Joseph, 1855.

The very famous portrait of Empress Elisabeth of Austria, painted by Franz Xavier Winterhalter in 1865. Fanatically attentive to her hair, face, figure, and dress, Elisabeth was once considered the most beautiful woman in all of Europe.

Portrait of Emperor Franz Joseph, also by artist Franz Xavier Winterhalter, 1865.

This lengthy feature article on the newly crowned empress appeared in the Illustrated London News, *Saturday, May 20, 1854. The article elaborated on her beauty and her family background, and it applauded the union of her and the emperor.*

This rendering of Elisabeth and Franz's royal wedding inside the Augustine Church in Vienna accompanied the article above.

A present-day photograph of Napoleon's Lombardian coronation carriage. Elisabeth made her wedding-day entrance in this carriage.

This scene, from a painting by Philipp Fleisher, depicts Elisabeth's extraordinary wedding procession. The gala procession covered several miles, here seen passing over the Elisabeth Bridge and the Vienna River before arriving at the Hofburg Palace.

Empress Elisabeth with Emperor Franz Joseph with two of their children, Princess Gisela and Crown Prince Rudolph, circa 1861.

Photograph of Prince Rudolph, circa 1880. He posed for this picture a year before he married Stephanie of Belgium.

Franz Joseph's mother, Archduchess Sophie. Also Elisabeth's aunt, she was less than pleased when Franz decided to marry Elisabeth over her "more suitable" sister, Helene.

Photograph of Elisabeth's mother, Princess Ludovica, taken in 1892, the year she died.

An 1874 photograph of Helene, Elisabeth's older sister, who was originally chosen by Archduchess Sophie to marry Emperor Franz Joseph.

Two of Elisabeth's younger sisters, Mathilde (top) and Sophie (bottom).

*Elisabeth's father, Maximilian
Joseph, Duke of Bavaria.
Elisabeth's love of poetry came
from her father, who was also
the composer of many
German songs.*

*Elisabeth's eldest brother,
Ludwig. Over the years,
Elisabeth became very close
to Ludwig's daughter,
Marie Larisch. Unfortunately,
their relationship proved to be
detrimental when Marie
released a book entitled
My Past, in which she wrote
numerous lies about
the Empress.*

Elisabeth's youngest brother,
Max Emmanuel.

Karl Theodor, Elisabeth's
favorite brother.

Map of Austria, circa 1853.

Photograph of Possenhofen as it appears today. Called "Possi" for short, the palace was the childhood home of Elisabeth. Built in 1536, it had many owners until Elisabeth's father, Duke Maximilian, bought it in 1834. Presently, Possenhofen is privately owned and closed to the public.

Hofburg Palace in Vienna. Though considerably smaller than Schönbrunn, this palace was equally gloomy and dismal for Elisabeth.

The Imperial Palace of Schönbrunn in Vienna, Austria. The grandiose Schönbrunn was reputed to have fourteen hundred and forty-one rooms.

Franz Joseph was born in this room at Schönbrunn Palace on August 18, 1830.

The bedroom once shared by Franz Joseph and Elisabeth at Schönbrunn, before their marriage became strained and they each occupied separate quarters.

Franz Joseph's chambers at Schönbrunn. Having no bathrooms, the room was equipped with a sink, pitchers, and basins for washing up.

This ivory miniature titled Elisabeth, the Equestrian *was painted by Karl Ritter von Kobierski. Renowned as an expert equestrian, the Empress spent much of her time in the 1870s and 1880s enjoying the sport of horseback riding. It is said that she would sometimes allow herself to be sewn into the tight-fitting bodice of her riding attire.*

Black court dress of the Empress Elisabeth of Austria, made by the court dressmaker, Fanni Scheiner. While lighter colors were worn during the first half of the century, black was thought to be more elegant towards the end of the 1800s.

Mourning dress of the Empress Elisabeth. Court practices notwithstanding, during the last years of her life, the Empress dressed almost exclusively in black, especially after the suicide of her son, Rudolph, in 1889, to express the deep mourning she felt over her loss.

The Empress and her lady-in-waiting, Countess Irma Grafin Sztaray, photographed in Geneva on September 3, 1898. It was Elisabeth's custom to travel publicly with the Countess or friends, unaccompanied by official escorts or bodyguards.

On September 10, 1898, while walking on the promenade of Lake Geneva with Countess Sztaray, the sixty-year-old Empress was tragically stabbed in the chest by a twenty-four-year-old Italian anarchist, Luigi Luccheni. This illustration titled Assassination of the Empress of Austria *depicts the event.*

This etching portrays the funeral services for the beloved Empress Elisabeth Amelie Eugenie of Austria, Queen of Hungary. On September 17, 1898, her remains were laid to rest in the imperial vault in Vienna.

Glossary of Characters

ELISABETH'S FAMILY

Duchess Ludovica, Royal Princess of Bavaria —
   Elisabeth's mother.

Duke Maximilian Joseph — Elisabeth's father.

Helene (Néné) — Elisabeth's older sister.

Ludwig — Elisabeth's oldest brother.

Karl Theodor — Elisabeth's brother.

Max Emmanuel — Elisabeth's brother.

Marie — Elisabeth's sister.

Mathilde — Elisabeth's sister.

Sophie — Elisabeth's youngest sister.

Franz Joseph I — Elisabeth's husband, Emperor
   of Austria.

Sophie, Archduchess of Austria — Elisabeth's aunt,
   her mother's sister. Mother of Franz Joseph I.

Archduke Karl Ludwig — brother of Franz Joseph I.

Queen Elise of Prussia — Elisabeth's aunt, her
   mother's sister.

ACQUAINTANCES AND ATTENDANTS

Baroness Wulfen — Elisabeth's governess.

Gustav — Sisi's valet.

Herr Ferdinand, or Nandl — Elisabeth's carriage attendant.

Fräulein Rödi — Elisabeth's lady-in-waiting.

Count Grunne — Emperor Franz Joseph's aide.

Count Májlath — Elisabeth's tutor.

Countess Esztherházy — Elisabeth's Mistress of the Robes.

FAMILY PETS

Punch — Elisabeth's horse.

About the Author

Barry Denenberg is the author of several critically acclaimed books for young readers, including five books in the Dear America series, *Mirror Mirror on the Wall: The Diary of Bess Brennan; Early Sunday Morning: The Pearl Harbor Diary of Amber Billows; When Will This Cruel War Be Over?: The Civil War Diary of Emma Simpson,* which was named an NCSS Notable Children's Trade Book in the Field of Social Studies and a YALSA Quick Pick; *One Eye Laughing, the Other Weeping: The Diary of Julie Weiss; So Far from Home: The Diary of Mary Driscoll, an Irish Mill Girl;* and two books in the My Name is America series, *The Journal of William Thomas Emerson: A Revolutionary War Patriot,* and *The Journal of Ben Uchida: Citizen 13599, Mirror Lake Internment Camp.* Praised for his meticulous research,

Barry Denenberg has written books about diverse times in American history, from the Civil War to Vietnam.

Denenberg says, "I first encountered the enigmatic and enchanting Empress of Austria while researching for the Dear America book *One Eye Laughing, The Other Weeping.* Even though her life and times weren't immediately relevant to that book, I found her so compelling that I read about her extensively. When my editor told me about The Royal Diaries, I knew this was my chance to justify spending even more time with this most complicated woman.

"Her extraordinary beauty, which was legendary, was complimented by her independent spirit and liberal political philosophy: characteristics of a woman born ahead of her time. She paid a dear price for her nonconformist ways.

"In this book, I have chosen to re-create the most dramatic moment in Sisi's (as she was called from an early age) life: her fabled meeting and subsequent marriage to the Emperor of Austria-Hungary, Franz Joseph.

"At the incredibly young age of sixteen, Sisi was now Elisabeth, Empress of a vast empire. Married to one of the most powerful men on earth at a critical time in history, she struggled mightily with her new role."

Denenberg's nonfiction works include *An American Hero: The True Story of Charles A. Lindbergh,* which was named an ALA Best Book for Young Adults, and a New York Public Library Book for the Teen Age; *Voices from Vietnam,* an ALA Best Book for Young Adults, a *Booklist* Editor's Choice, and a New York Public Library Book for the Teen Age; and *All Shook Up: The Life and Death of Elvis Presley.* He lives with his wife and their daughter in Westchester County, New York.

Acknowledgments

The author would like to thank Kerry Balassone, Kristen Eberle, Amy Griffin, Sonia Black, Lisa Sandell, Hara Lewis, Manuela Soares, and Kerrie Baldwin.

Cover painting by Tim O'Brien

Page 120: Elisabeth, Brown Brothers, Sterling, Pennsylvania.

Page 121: Franz Joseph, Culver Pictures, New York, New York.

Page 122: Winterhalter painting of Elisabeth, Art History Museum (Kunsthistorisches Museum), Vienna, Austria.

Page 123: Winterhalter painting of Franz Joseph, Art History Museum (Kunsthistorisches Museum), Vienna, Austria.

Page 124 (top): London article featuring Elisabeth, Culver Pictures, New York, New York.

Page 124 (bottom): London article featuring royal wedding, Culver Pictures, New York, New York.

Page 125 (top): Elisabeth's wedding carriage, Art History Museum (Kunsthistorisches Museum), Vienna, Austria.

Page 125 (bottom): Royal wedding procession, Austrian National Library, Bildarchiv, Vienna, Austria.

Page 126: Elisabeth, Franz Joseph, Gisela, and Rudolph, Austrian National Library, Bildarchiv, Vienna, Austria.

Page 127: Rudolph, Hulton Archive, Getty Images, New York, New York.

Page 128: Archduchess Sophie, Austrian Archives/CORBIS.

Page 129: Ludovica, Austrian National Library, Bildarchiv, Vienna, Austria.

Page 130: Helene, Austrian National Library, Bildarchiv, Vienna, Austria.

Page 131 (top): Mathilde, Austrian National Library, Bildarchiv, Vienna, Austria.

Page 131 (bottom): Sophie, Austrian National Library, Bildarchiv, Vienna, Austria.

Page 132 (top): Maximilian, Austrian National Library, Bildarchiv, Vienna, Austria.

Page 132 (bottom): Ludwig, Austrian National Library, Bildarchiv, Vienna, Austria.

Page 133 (top): Max Emmanuel, Austrian National Library, Bildarchiv, Vienna, Austria.

Page 133 (bottom): Karl Theodor, Austrian National Library, Bildarchiv, Vienna, Austria.

Page 134: Map of Austria, James McMahon.

Page 135 (top): Possenhofen, Geoffrey Harrison, Leicester, U.K.

Page 135 (bottom): Hofburg Palace, Austrian National Tourism Office, Vienna, Austria.

Page 136 (top): Schönbrunn, Schönbrunn Palace, Vienna, Austria.

Page 136 (bottom): Room where Franz Joseph was born, Brown Brothers, Sterling, Pennsylvania.

Page 137 (top): Franz and Elisabeth's bedroom, Austrian National Library, Bildarchiv, Vienna, Austria.

Other books in The Royal Diaries series

ELIZABETH I
Red Rose of the House of Tudor
by Kathryn Lasky

CLEOPATRA VII
Daughter of the Nile
by Kristiana Gregory

MARIE ANTOINETTE
Princess of Versailles
by Kathryn Lasky

ISABEL
Jewel of Castilla
by Carolyn Meyer

ANASTASIA
The Last Grand Duchess
by Carolyn Meyer

NZINGHA
Warrior Queen of Matamba
by Patricia C. McKissack

Copyright © 2003 by Barry Denenberg

All rights reserved. Published by Scholastic Inc.
557 Broadway, New York, New York 10012.
SCHOLASTIC, THE ROYAL DIARIES, and associated logos are trademarks
and/or registered trademarks of Scholastic Inc.

Library of Congress Cataloging-in-Publication Data
Denenberg, Barry
Elisabeth : the princess bride / by Barry Denenberg.
p.   cm. — (The Royal Diaries)
Summary: The diary of Princess Elisabeth, written in 1853–1854,
describing her engagement and marriage to her cousin Franz Joseph I,
Emperor of Austria. Includes historical notes concerning her life as Empress.
ISBN 0-439-26644-0 (alk. paper)
[I. Elisabeth, Empress, consort of Franz Joseph I, Emperor of Austria
1837–1898 — Juvenile fiction.   II. Elisabeth, Empress, consort of
Franz Joseph I, Emperor of Austria 1837–1898 — Fiction.   III. Princesses —
Fiction.   IV. Diaries.   V. Austria — History — 1848–1867 — Juvenile
fiction.   VI. Austria — History — 1848–1867 — Fiction.
PZ7.D4135 El 2003
[Fic] 21   2002070818
CIP AC
10   9   8   7   6   5   4   3   03   04   05   06   07

The display type was set in Callifonts E49.
The text type was set in Augereau.
Book design by Elizabeth B. Parisi
Photo research by Amla Sanghvi and Sarah-Maria Vischer-Masino

Printed in the U.S.A.   23
First edition, April 2003